And when you see a man being led by a woman down the street toward Aunt Abigail's, you might hear her say: "Finally, I'm going to see you trimmed like I've wanted for so long!"

All men secretly yearn to be trimmed. Otherwise, why do they always have such big erections when they're strapped into Aunt Abigail's special chair ready to be trimmed? Aunt Abigail always notices the guy's erection and takes pity on him and lets him jerk off one last time while she and the ladies watch, laughing and teasing. But after he has a big cum and he sees Aunt Abigail sharpening her shears then he starts begging her not to do it, which makes the ladies laugh even more. Then, when Aunt Abigail starts snipping into his manhood pouch the guy always starts squealing in terror and panic. The newspaper account always describes how much squealing the guy did.

3. BRIDGE NIGHT DEMO

It was the night of Alison's weekly bridge club meeting. The club met every week n Alison's living room. During the bridge game, Alison's house husband, Little Billy, always waited on Alison and her girlfriends, bringing pitchers of daiquiris and other refreshments. Little Billy hadn't had a job in years, not since marrying Alison. Alison was a high-powered marketing consultant, and her income was more than sufficient to keep them both in style. And Alison liked keeping Little Billy around the house, and she relished keeping him as her own personal, private little plaything.

Alison always insisted that Little Billy wear tight shorts while waiting on them. The shorts were very revealing and really showed off his cute little butt. As Little Billy moved around the bridge table, waiting on them, Alison's girlfriends just couldn't resist occasionally giving his cute little butt a playful pat, or slap, or even a quick, sharp little goose.

The first time Alison's best friend, Georgina, goosed Little Billy during a bridge game, he jumped and squeaked and then let out a loud "oooohhhhhh!" The girls all laughed heartily at that. "Wow!" said Georgina, "Little Billy really seems to have an especially sensitive little backside, there."

"Oh yes," laughed Alison, "Little Billy's always been very sensitive back there, but he's become even more sensitive in the past 3 months. Haven't you, Little Billy?"

Little Billy just blushed deep red, and said, "Oh please, Alison, stop it, you're embarrassing me!" And he then rushed off to the kitchen. Alison and her friends all laughed at Little Billy's effeminate display of girlish embarrassment.

"Really, girls," said Alison, "he is amazing, the responses he has down there, if you know what I mean. About 3 months ago, I started to really work on boosting his

awareness down there and to really open up his receptivity in that area, and the results have been just incredible!"

Alison's girlfriends responded to this with blank stares and a few titters. Georgina spoke up and said, "what are we talking about here, exactly, Alison? I assume you're referring to bedroom activities, correct?"

"Yes, that's right," said Alison, "I thought my meaning was clear, sorry. Yes, I've been working on Little Billy's backdoor responses in the bedroom, and it's been a real eye opener, I can tell you, he! he! And that's not all that's been opened, he! he! I've really been able to get Little Billy to open up to a whole new side of himself. Wide open, so to speak, he! he!"

"Oh Alison, I must say," said Georgina, "you're almost as bad as a man, sometimes, bragging about your sex life. You're been hinting around for ages about all the cool things you've trained Little Billy to do. Well I think that if you're so darn proud of him, why don't we schedule a special club meeting dedicated to you giving us all a no-holds-barred show of your little hubby's special talents?"

This suggestion silenced Alison for the time being. She'd been quite taken aback, at first, by the suggestion that she put her bedroom love making practices on public display. The girls continued to play bridge, and the discussion moved on to other topics, but Alison's mind couldn't help returning to toy with Georgina's bold suggestion. Just then, Little Billy came trotting into the room with another pitcher of daiquiris and said, "Hey Girls, what're you all talking about?" The girls all warmly returned his greeting. After all, they all really did like him, even if they mostly couldn't help looking down on him as just a silly little plaything. Then, Little Billy looked over at his wife and was puzzled by the strange glint he saw in her eye, and a mysterious little smirk that played at the corners of her mouth.

Two week later, Little Billy was cleaning up, getting everything ready for that night's bridge club meeting. Little Billy was vacuuming in the living room and Alison was freshening up in the bathroom, when they both heard the front doorbell ring. Alison had just gotten home from work, and Billy was still wearing the frilly pink apron that he wore around the house while doing his housekeeping chores.

The doorbell rang again. "Could you get that, Little Billy?" yelled Alison from her bedroom. They slept in separate bedrooms, and Alison only allowed Little Billy to join her in her bedroom when she needed to use him to satisfy her sexual appetites in some way or other.

Little Billy answered the door. As expected, it was Georgina, Lydia and Carol. They all lived nearby and often joined each other for the walk over to Alison's. They all greeted Little Billy warmly, and he ushered them into the living room to sit down

Soon, Alison came out of bathroom and joined them.

. AMAZON BAR

I'd heard about the goings on at the Amazon bar and they frightened and excited ne. I finally worked up the courage to go. Soon, the big, luscious Amazons had me tripped naked and were using me as their sexual plaything.

When I need to take a bathroom break the Amazons direct me to a short hallway t the back of the bar. They warn me to be careful which room I go into or I might et more than I bargained on, and then they laugh knowingly.

After I take a leak and come back out into the hallway I notice an open doorway a ouple doors down. The light's on in the room and I hear strange noises coming from . I tiptoe down and take a quick peek. I can't believe what I see.

In the room, a naked young man is lying on a medical exam table with his feet in e stirrups and his legs spread wide. He has an erection which he's busy jerking off. big, luscious Amazon wearing only a corset is standing between his legs and is ulling one of his testicles out of an incision in his sac and is getting ready to snip the ord with surgical scissors. This turns me on so much that my cock is rock hard and I nmediately grab it to jerk off.

The Amazon catches me peeking and smiles and invites me to come in and have closer look. I'm shy and embarrassed but I accept her invitation. "Welcome to the ipping room," she says warmly. She tells me to keep masturbating. Then she turns er attention back to the boy. She purrs and coos to him as she continues working etween his legs.

She's totally relaxed and casual and acts like it's the most natural thing in the orld. The young man pants and gasps and looks up at the Amazon with total love d devotion. I stand and watch as the Amazon snips the second cord and he cums a cket load. She smiles down at my hand on my cock and tells me she's glad I'm still asturbating, it keeps me in the mood.

After she sews up the boy's sac she tells him he can go now. He thanks her, gets wn off the table and leaves. Then the Amazon smiles and tells me it's my turn. I sitate and she asks me how my nuts feel, do they ache? I admit they do. She iles and says, "You know what they're aching for, don't you?" she asks. She tells to climb up onto the table so she can get started. I realize she's right and so I do she says. She tells me to start masturbating again.

As she begins to work on my sac she says softly, "What a dear, sweet young man are to give me such an important part of yourself." A few minutes later she snips second cord and I cum a bucket load.

A little later while she sews me up I notice the shelves on the wall have small jars them with a pair of testicles in each. She tells me how she loves to look at her

trophies and think about how there are men walking around the town with empty sacs between their legs because she has taken their balls. Then she tells me I can leave. I thank her and go.

When I get back into the main room the Amazons notice my sad, empty sac drooping down. They laugh and say they told me so. I just hang my head in shame, get dressed and leave the bar.

2. AUNT ABIGAIL'S TRIMMIN' PARLOR

Aunt Abigail runs a beauty parlor for the ladies and in the back she runs a speci 'trimmin' parlor' for the men.

The town's completely run by women. There's a special town ordinance that allows a woman to bring a man in for trimmin' if she sees fit. Women bring in their co-workers, boyfriends, husbands, fathers, brothers, uncles, granddads, cousins, sons, in-laws and neighbors.

If a lady catches a guy cheatin', exposin' himself or jerkin' off, she brings him int Aunt Abigail's for a quick little 'trim' down in between his legs.

Aunt Abigail takes him in the back room and gets him naked and puts him in he special trimmin' chair with his legs spread nice and wide. Then she tells him since h hasn't been makin' proper use of his manly equipment she's gonna trim it with her special shears. The ladies who bring a man in always stay to watch - they love to watch a man being trimmed.

To add to their shame and embarrassment the local paper (run by women, of course) prints a list every week of the men who've been trimmed along with their offense. It's truly devastating for a man to have the whole town know he's been castrated for jerking off. The other men don't say anything, especially if they've be trimmed too, but the women mercilessly tease a newly trimmed man. All men are required to wear a bright pink armband in public for a month after being trimmed

The most common offense cited is jerking off. This has led to some abuse since some of the women deliberately tease and excite a man in order to trick him into jerking off. They just love to catch a man with his 'pants down'. When they bring h into Aunt Abigail's they laugh and say, "Look who we caught red-handed!" Aunt Abigail laughs too and says, "Uh oh, you've been a naughty boy! You know what happens to naughty boys who play with themselves!" Then she proceeds to trim h while the ladies watch with much amusement and delight.

It's common to hear a woman say to a man in public: "I'll see you trimmed one these days, mister, just you wait!"

Once they were all comfortable, Georgina asked, with a wicked little smirk, "Have ou told him yet, Alison?"

Little Billy froze in the middle of what he was doing and asked, with mounting error, "Told me? Told me what, Alison? What haven't you told me? Please tell me, lison, please!"

The girls all laughed at Little Billy's bleating desperation and Alison said, "Now ittle Billy, you know better than to get yourself all excited about things before you now exactly what they are."

"But, but, but," stammered Little Billy, "you, you, you promised, you promised ne, Alison, that you wouldn't do any more of those things to me that you used to o. You, you know those things, Alison. Alison, please! I beg of you, what are you up o? Please tell me what's going to happen to me! Please tell it's not going to be omething humiliating or embarrassing! Please!"

"Uh oh," said Alison smugly, "here we go again. Little Billy's getting himself all vorked up into one of his little states. Now just calm down Little Billy, and try and et a grip on yourself, OK? Let's try and look at things rationally, shall we? I know ou're not used to thinking rationally, but let's give it a try anyway, just for the ovelty, Ok? First off, we all know that you're my little house husband, that you're ny property and are entirely mine to do with as I please, don't we?"

"Yes, Alison," whimpered Little Billy.

"Secondly," said Alison, "you know that, no matter what I do, and however much ou may find the things I do to you to be strange or uncomfortable, that I always ave your welfare and best interests at heart, don't I?"

"Yes, Alison," Little Billy whimpered again.

"Then you have absolutely nothing to worry about, do you, Little Billy?" asked lison, with a sly wink to her friends. "Now stop being so silly and go and get us a itcher of daiquiris," commanded Alison.

After the girls had each had a couple daiquiris and been chatting together for a hile, Alison said, "Well, I don't know about you girls, but those daiquiris really hit ne spot. I'm feeling nice and loose now, and a little bit horny, to tell the truth. I ould definitely do with some loving attention from my cute little house husband. Vhat do you say, Little Billy? Are you in the mood to give me a little lovin'?"

"Please Alison," said Little Billy in a soft urgent voice, "don't talk like that in front f company. You're starting to embarrass me."

But Alison just ignored him, and, leaning back on the couch, stuck her butt out ver the end of the cushion, hiked up her skirt, and pulled off her panties.

Little Billy shrieked when he saw what Alison was doing and ran, terrified, to hid in the kitchen.

Alison apologized to her friends and said, "Well, it looks like now I'll have to go and get Little Billy straightened out. Please bear with me, girls, it'll only take me a couple of minutes." Then she got up and headed off to the kitchen. The girls could hear Alison talking in a low, firm voice, and Little Billy responding in terrified little squeaks and bleats. Then, Alison burst through the kitchen door, marching quickly t the bedroom, with Little Billy in tow.

From the bedroom, the girls heard nothing for a moment, and then they began to hear a series of smacks, while Alison's voice spoke in a low, lecturing tone. Soon, the smacks stopped, and Alison and Little Billy reappeared. Little Billy's face was ve red and tear streaked, and his lower lip trembled as he gingerly rubbed his bottom with both hands.

"OK, Little Billy," said Alison, "are you ready now to do as you're told?"

"Yes, dear," said Little Billy in a small, frightened voice.

Alison sat back down on the couch, leaned back and hiked up her skirt, exposing her hot, wet pussy. "OK Little Billy," said Alison, "come over here and get down on your knees and show my friends here what a good little pussy licker you are."

Then Alison stopped and said, "Wait a minute, I almost forgot. Whenever I make Little Billy go down and serve me with his mouth, it never fails that his little peepee gets very stiff and excited, as well. Isn't that right, Little Billy?"

"Oh please, Alison, please, I beg of you, no more humiliation!" whined Little Billy

"I'll take that answer as a 'yes'," said Alison, and she and her friends all laughed.

"So, to help make Little Billy feel a little less constrained while he's paying oral tribute to me, I always let him diddle his little peepee while he's licking me. Isn't tha right, Little Billy?"

Little Billy saw that there was no point in trying to object, so he just stood there in silence and blushed deep red from his collar all the way to the roots of his hair.

"Yup," said Alison, "so now is no different. And you know what that means, don you, Little Billy? Take off all your clothes except your t-shirt." Then she said to her friends, "I let him keep his little t-shirt on for warmth and security, you know." Turning back to Little Billy, Alison added, "But remember, Little Billy, while you're playing with your little peepee, be very careful not to get too carried away and hav a naughty little accident, Ok? You know you're only allowed to have little accidents when I give you my express permission, don't you?"

Little Billy did as he was told and was soon standing in the middle of the living oom, naked except for his t-shirt.

Then, Alison leaned back luxuriantly on the couch, naked from the waist down, nd spread her legs wide apart and beckoned Little Billy to come over to her. Her oft, furry pussy was thrust shamelessly up towards him. Little Billy looked down on is wife's soft, glowing sex, it's moist pink lips slightly parted, and he could smell it's angy sweet musk rise up to where he stood. The smell of his powerful, dynamic ife's sweet pussy had its usual effect on him, and his little peepee started surging nd ballooning up to a state of throbbing stiffness.

As Little Billy stood there, mesmerized, looking down at his wife's musky sex, he elt a sudden impulse to fall on top of her and to thrust his yearning hardness deep p into her soft warm belly. But she had trained him too well for that. In fact, Alison ad, for as long as they had known each other, never given Little Billy permission to enetrate her. Little Billy had, on a couple occasions, shyly and pleadingly asked her allow him to, but Alison just laughed it off as preposterous. "Don't be silly, you ould never give me any real pleasure with that little nubber of yours, Little Billy," lison had said, "so you might as well just forget about it, OK?"

Meanwhile, Alison was getting tired of waiting with her legs wide open, and said, 'mon, Little Billy, quit daydreaming and get down on your knees and start giving y pussy some attention. If you keep me waiting too much longer, my poor little ussy might catch cold."

While Alison's friends watched, Little Billy got down on his knees between his ife's legs and bent over, bringing his face down close to her pussy. Her pussy was nly an inch from his face and it's heavy, musky odor overpowered him. He stared at e soft pink flesh, the mossy fur, the slightly glistening lips, as if in a trance.

"C'mon," said Alison with a giggle, "don't keep me and my friends waiting. I'm ying to feel you work your magic, and my friends are anxious to see how a real pro e you performs. I told them how good you were at it, and how much you enjoy oing it. So don't just sit there and breathe on it, get down on it and start licking!"

Burning with shame and humiliation at being made to do this very private and ery submissive thing for the entertainment of his wife's friends, Little Billy bent rwards and gingerly pressed his mouth against his wife's hot, steamy moistness.

As Alison and her friends waited and watched in breathless anticipation, Little lly slowly began to lick his wife's sweet pussy lips. As he did so, his right hand tomatically began, just as it always did when he began to service his wife, to reach etween his legs and curl its fingers eagerly around his aching peepee. Little Billy egan to push his face more forcefully into his wife's steamy sex, and to lick more gressively. As the sensations began to overwhelm her, Alison threw back her head nd abandoned herself to Little Billy's aggressive licking. Alison's friends leaned

forward, smiling and giggling as they watched Little Billy eagerly perform this submissive sexual service for his wife. And Little Billy, forgetting for the moment where he was, began to enjoy the sensations of pleasuring his wife, combined with the wonderful feelings he was giving himself with his hand as he slowly, but firmly, stroked himself.

Soon, Alison was grasping Little Billy by the back of the head and forcefully pulling his face into her crotch, her hips bucking wildly as she started to cum.

After Alison was done cumming, she released her hold on Little Billy's head and let him come up for air. He did so, gasping and sputtering, his whole face slimy and dripping from the byproducts of the crude, animal pleasure that his wife had derive from his submissive oral tribute.

"Run and fetch me a towel, won't you, Little Billy," said Alison, in an offhand wa "Oh, and while you're at it, why don't you try and do something about all that gunk on your face, too, OK? Really, Little Billy, you are a sight, he! he!"

As Little Billy turned to go to the bathroom, Alison turned to her friends and sai "see, I told you he was a great little pussy eater. Pretty impressive, huh?"

Alison's friends all agreed that what they had seen was an outstanding performance. Alison said, "Georgina, you look a little flustered. It looks to me like maybe you got a little carried away while watching Little Billy's performance. In fac I'd be willing to bet you'd like to try a little sample of that for yourself, wouldn't you?"

Georgina blushed, and said in a soft sexy voice, "Really, Alison, you are just too much sometimes! But seriously, it did look absolutely heavenly what he was doing for you down there. I'd be lying if I told you I wasn't thinking about what it would feel like to have the same thing done to me."

"Ha! Ha! You're a dirty little vixen after my own heart," said Alison, "and in case any of you haven't already guessed, tonight is 'Ladies Night', and Little Billy is available to be freely used by each and every one of you in any way you like, he! he!"

Little Billy was almost to the bathroom when he heard his wife in the next roon offering his sexual services to her friends. He blanched white with fear, almost stumbled, and then, regaining his balance, continued shakily on into the bathroom As he began to wash himself up, his mind was a whirling turmoil of dread and anxiety.

As Little Billy cautiously returned to the living room, he was terrified to see that Georgina had replaced his wife in the middle of the sofa, and had removed her panties and hiked up her skirt to reveal her moist, mossy pussy. The girls noticed

Little Billy standing at the entrance to the living room, staring at Georgina's pussy, stricken with fear, and this caused them all to laugh uproariously. Little Billy hoped it was all just a joke, but when he looked over at his wife, the stern, commanding expression on her face told him otherwise.

Soon, Little Billy was on his knees in front of Georgina, nervously taking in the different look and smell of her hot, moist love box. Alison told Little Billy to stop screwing around and get to work, and so he meekly bent his head and started paying Georgina the same kind of oral tribute as he had to his wife a few minutes before.

After Georgina had had a nice, big, satisfying orgasm, Alison stood up and announced: "OK, girls, and now for the treat you've all been waiting for, the main event of the evening." Then, turning to Little Billy, she said, "Little Billy, I want you to go and run into my bedroom and fetch your knee pads, the bottle of lubricant, and my strap-on, OK honey?"

Little Billy couldn't believe what he was hearing. He stood stock still, paralyzed with shock and

fear, staring wide-eyed, his mouth hanging open, at his wife. Alison leaned back on the couch and coolly met his gaze, a smug knowing smirk playing over her lips. "C'mon, Little Billy, mustn't keep the girls waiting. I've been telling them all about how much you love the way I make love to you, and they're just dying for a demonstration. So, be a good little boy and run quick like a bunny and fetch the things I told you."

Soon, Alison was stepping into the strap-on harness and pulling it up to her waist where she buckled it firmly into place. Her friends complemented her on how she looked. "Looks very good on you," said Georgina, "very natural." Alison gave a snort and said, "Thanks, babe." Alison then re-adjusted the straps to position the base of the dildo so that it was pressing on her clit, just the way she liked it.

"OK, Little Billy," said Alison. "Get up onto the coffee table and assume the position."

Little Billy got up onto the table and got into the supremely submissive position: on his knees, with his legs spread wide apart, and his chest and chin down on the table.

The girls couldn't suppress their hysterical laughter as they watched Little Billy get into this totally humiliating and submissive posture. He looked just like a horny little slut bending over and itching to be taken doggy style.

Alison stopped a moment to fully savor the delicious sight of Little Billy offering his sweet, puckered little bottom hole so submissively to her. She stroked his soft, pinkish, slightly parted bottom cheeks. Then she brought her hand down between

his legs to lightly caress his tight, wrinkly, hairless little scrotum. Billy let out a sigh o pleasure and delight at Alison's gentle handling of his sensitive little ball sac. Alison insisted that he always keep it clean shaven. There was something about seeing his pink, nude little sac that she just found very cute and sexy.

Alison then lubricated the dildo, and then spread lubricant up and down Little Billy's enticingly parted cleft. Little Billy squirmed and whimpered as she gently spread it up and down his cleft, and then he gasped and moaned when she slowly inserted one slippery index finger into his tight and tender bottom hole, and pushe it all the way inside.

Alison's girlfriends all had a perfect view of what she was doing to her little hous husband. They all giggled as they watched her slowly begin to slide her finder in an out of him and watched him squirming and whimpering with helpless pleasure in response to what she was doing to him.

"Hmmmm, you like this don't you, Little Billy, you, bad, dirty little boy, you," Alison said, as she continued to slowly finger fuck her husband's tight, quivering ass "Uhhhhhh, ohhhhhhh, ahhhhhhh," was all Little Billy could manage in response.

"Just look how the little slut responds to my finger," said Alison. "Such a dirty, nasty, bad little boy to enjoy having this done to him, yes you are, you bad, bad, little boy."

Turning to her friends, Alison laughed and said, "If you think this is bad, you should see what he does when I slip the dildo up into him."

Suiting her actions to her words, Alison removed her finger and wiped it on a small hand towel. Then she stepped forward and brought the tip of the dildo right up next to Little Billy's tight, puckered bottom hole. Billy felt the dildo pressing against his most sensitive spot and a slight tremor of anticipatory pleasure ran through him.

Alison grasped Little Billy firmly by the hips and slowly began to slide the dildo u into him. Little Billy gave a long deep groan as he felt the hard plastic penis begin sliding up inside him. When it was only half way in, Little Billy couldn't prevent himself from wriggling excitedly and eagerly pushing back towards Alison, anxious and impatient to get himself fully impaled on Alison's big plastic penis.

Soon it was all the way up and Little Billy felt the fleshy warmth of his wife's fir muscular hips pressing against his bottom. Little Billy sighed and moaned with satisfaction as his wife slowly ground the dildo deep into him with a small circular motion of her hips. "Just look at the little slut," said Alison to her amazed and delighted friends, "Just see how shameless he is! Can you believe it was only 3 months ago that I first took his cherry?"

"Little Billy likes to have his little bottom fucked, doesn't he?" Alison said to Little illy as she started to slowly piston the dildo in and out his tight, squirmy little ottom hole.

"Oh Alison," responded Little Billy, "oh Alison, you know I love the things you do o me, oh, oh, that feels sooooooo good!"

"Yes," said Alison, "he likes it so much, I've been wondering how he'd respond to he real thing. What do you think, Little Billy? I'll bet you're dying to find out how a ig hard cock feels pumping in and out of your tight little hole, aren't you?

"Oh no!" squealed Little Billy, "That's not funny, Alison, please don't joke about hat," and then he started moaning again, "Ooooooh, ooooh, oooh, god, that feels o good."

"Who's joking?" asked Alison, with a devilish smile, "I'd just love to see you down n your hands and knees, your butt high in the air, with a big hard cock pumping in nd out of your tight little bottom. I bet that'd really make you squeal. And I bet if ou wriggled your bottom real nice and sexy, you could even make him shoot all of is hot gooey cum up inside you."

All Little Billy could manage in response was to moan and say, "nooooo, leeeeeeeaaaaaseeee, nooooooooo, ooooooh, ummmmmm, ahhhhhhhh!"

"Hey Georgina," said Alison, "do me a favor and take a peek between Little Billy's gs for me would you, please? Is his little peepee standing at attention yet?"

Georgina did as she was asked and then said, "Yup, the little thing is just as hard nd red and shiny as anything."

"OK, Little Billy," said Alison, "you've been a good boy, so you now have my ermission to play with you little peepee some more." Little Billy didn't' need to be old twice. In a split second, his hand flew up to grab his stiff cock and to start igorously stroking it.

Little Billy moaned and whimpered like a slutty little girl while Alison pumped the ildo in and out of him. She savored the sexy way the base of the dildo stimulated er clit. After about 15 minutes, Alison was satisfied and she pulled the dildo out of im, unbuckled the harness, and slid it down off her. She told Little Billy to stand up, anded him the strap-on and told him to go to the bathroom and clean himself up nd to clean the dildo and put it away. After he was done with that, she instructed im to come right back.

The girls chatted for a few minutes while Little Billy was busy doing his clean up hores. Soon, he was back in the living room, as attentive and obedient as ever, but lso a little nervous about what to expect from Alison next.

"OK girls," said Alison, "since Little Billy has been such a good boy all night and has put on such a hot, sexy show for us all, I think it's only fair that he be given a little reward, don't you?"

"Well," said Georgina, "to tell you the truth, Alison, it's running a little late, and I've got a big meeting first thing tomorrow morning. Maybe we should just call it a night, and you can give Little Billy his reward after we leave?"

"Aww," said Alison, "don't be that way! What a party pooper! Come on, it'll only take a minute, and I'm sure you'll all find it very entertaining." Then, turning to Littl Billy, she said, "OK, Little Billy, I want you to sit on the coffee table, facing the girls and show them how a dirty little boy like you plays with his peepee until all of his hot, sloppy boy juice squirts out, OK?"

Little Billy was mortified, yet again, to hear his wife treat another of his private sexual activities as a matter for public entertainment, but he knew that it was useless to argue with her.

Little Billy did as he was told and was soon pumping his hand vigorously in his la in front of the girls as they giggled and made catty remarks about what a little sissy he was, and about how it looked as if he'd done this to himself many, many times before.

"Oh yes," confirmed Alison, "Little Billy's practically a career masturbator, aren't you, Little Billy? He! He! He loves to play with himself so much, it's really starting to become a nuisance around the house. I'm forever catching him at it, in the bathroom, or in his bedroom, or sometimes, even in the kitchen while he's making supper!" The girls all laughed hysterically at that.

"Oh please don't make fun of me, Alison," pleaded Little Billy while he continue to stroke his bursting cock in front of them, "I know I play with myself too much, an I try to be good, but I can't help it. I'm home all alone all day and I start to think off some of the sexy things you do to me, and that makes my little peepee get awfully stiff, and I just can't help it, I have to run and pull my pants down and sit right dowr and grab it and start stroking it and oh god, it feels so good, oh, oh, please, Alison, oh, oh, you make me do it, you make me do it!"

The girls all giggled and laughed at Little Billy as he made such a helpless spectacle of his most private feelings.

"It's gotten to be such a problem," continued Alison, "that I've been shopping around for a good chastity device that I can lock him up into during the day while I' at work. Honestly, it gotten to the point where, when I come home, I inspect his little peepee and it's all red, rough and sore from all the rubbing. And if I want to us him later on in the bedroom for oral tribute, or give him a good hard buttfucking, h little peepee hardly even stands at attention because he's used up all his seed

laying with himself."

"No! No! Please don't do that, Alison!" begged Little Billy, "Please don't lock up y little peepee so I can't play with it anymore! Please!"

The girls all laughed heartily at Little Billy's anxiety and desperation.

Alison noticed that Little Billy was almost ready to cum. "In fact, girls, I've even een considering a more drastic solution that would greatly reduce the time and ess involved with catering to his peepee's constant demands for attention. One of ur dogs needs to be neutered next week, and I've been toying with the idea of alling the vet and asking her to make a house call. After she's done doing the dog," lison paused and watched Little Billy, as his fist was a blur in his lap, and then, as e first drops started to arc out of the end of his prick she continued, "after she's one doing the dog, I expect, it would be a simple matter for her to do Little Billy, o."

"NO!" shrieked Little Billy as his sperm erupted from his cock, "Oh no, Alison, no, ease, please don't have me neutered, please, oh, oh, it feels so good to play with yself, oh oh, you make me do it, you make me feel so hot and excited, I can't help , I can't help it, you make me do it, you make me! Ohhhhh!"

As Little Billy's cum continued to squirt out, Alison replied, "Yes, Little Billy, you now that that is exactly what you deserve, you're such a bad, dirty little boy, you eserve to have you silly little nuts clipped off by the vet, just like a dirty little doggy. 'd be such fun, I could show off your new ball-less scrotum to the bridge club and e could all laugh at how you still always put your hand in your lap to jerk off, but matter how hard you try, you can't get a little stiffy anymore. Ha! Ha!"

Little Billy's cock was only oozing cum now and he sat back, exhausted, and himpered in a small, resigned voice, "No, no, Alison, no, please, please don't have e neutered like a dirty little doggy, please, please, I'll be good, I promise, oh ease, please believe me, I'll do it this time, I'll control my urges, you'll see, just give e a chance, just one more chance, please."

"Oh stop whining, Little Billy," snapped Alison in mock anger, "really, you are just ich a little baby sometimes. Now, go and wash all that gunky spunk off yourself, id then come back and try and get it up off the table and the carpet too. Go! Now! iop! Chop!"

While Little Billy was in the bathroom getting himself washed up, Alison turned her friends and confided, "You know, girls, do you remember what I was saying rlier to Little Billy about bringing home a man to give him a taste of what a real ck feels like? Well, there's a big handsome gay guy at work named Jake, and I owed him a couple videos I made of Little Billy while I was putting him through his ices in the bedroom, both orally and anally, and Jake's says he can't wait to feel

Little Billy's hot mouth on his cock, or to hear Little Billy squeal as he slides his big hard cock up Little Billy's squirmy little bottom hole for the first time. Jake even confessed to me that he's already started getting into the habit of jerking off while fantasizing about how hot and satisfying it's going to be to use Little Billy for his pleasure in a long, hot suck and fuck session."

Just then, Little Billy returned from the bathroom with a sponge, a small bucket of soapy water and some paper towels. He had also taken the liberty of putting his shorts back on. "What're you girls talking about?" asked Little Billy in a warm and cheerful voice.

"Oh, nothing," said Alison, giving her friends significant glances and smiling devilishly. Then turning to face Little Billy, she continued, "we were just trying to decide what might be the most entertaining activities and things to do at the next little surprise party we hold in your honor, Little Billy."

"What!?" squeaked Little Billy. "Oh no, please, not another one, oh no, please, no, please don't do that Alison, ladies, please, please don't do it, don't do any more of those things to me while everybody watches, oh please, no please, don't do it, don't do it, don't do it to me! Please!"

The girls all shot significant glances at each other and rocked back in their seats and laughed and laughed very heartily for a very long time.

4. CASTRATION FARM

One day, I was doing my laundry in the apartment building laundry room when Sharon and Alison, two hot young vixens, came in. They were both wearing cut-offs and tight t-shirts and no bras. They giggled when they caught me ogling their jiggly little titties. Sharon asked me if I would like to drive them up to Alison's aunt's farm the next weekend. They giggled as I stuttered out that I'd love to.

On the drive up we all sat in the front seat. Since it was a hot summer day the girls decided to take off their t-shirts. They giggled when they saw the big bulge in my crotch made by the hard-on I got looking over at their perky titties. Alison told me I'd better do something to relieve that swelling between my legs or we were going to have an accident. The girls told me to turn off onto a deserted dirt road ar stop the car. With a sly smile Sharon looked at me and said, “I bet you really wanna to grab your stiff penis and jerk off, don't you?” I just gulped and blushed and look away. Alison smugly said, “I thought so. So why don't you do that? Go ahead and pull off your shorts and give us a show?” They giggled as I hurried to comply. Soon, was urgently stroking myself right in front of them. It was intensely embarrassing but I couldn't help myself. Sharon said she thought I was being very dirty and I should be ashamed of myself for jerking off like that. Alison agreed and said she

stocks. A few minutes later she starting deftly snipping into my tender, defenseless little scrotal sac. I started squealing and the girls started giggling.

As she was sewing me back up Aunt Cassie thanked me for coming to visit her farm. I just whimpered and the girls snickered.

5. CASTRATION SLUT

A college boy stands waiting at a bus stop. He bends over to pick up a copy of the latest issue of the weekly campus newspaper lying on the sidewalk. There's a story on the front page about a rash of mysterious castrations on campus. A photo accompanies the article that shows a forlorn set of male genitals. The penis is held up out of the way so that the slack, empty sac can be clearly seen.

He is approached by an attractive brunette in her mid-30s wearing a dark, conservative business skirt-suit. She introduces herself and tells him she's a journalist. She asks him if he would like to help her with some research for an article she's working on. He asks her what it's about. She smiles warmly and says the article is all about the various different ways young men do 'it', and she holds her right hand up and makes the unmistakable jerk-off gesture.

He blushes and stammers, "But I..."

"You do do it, don't you?" she asks. "Don't be embarrassed. All men do."

He blushes, looks down and gulps, "Uh huh, I, I guess so."

"I thought so," she says with a sly smile. "What I want you to do is to come with me to my apartment. You'll take off your clothes, sit down and do it while I watch."

"But, would I, would I have to...," he stammers some more.

"Have an orgasm and ejaculate?" she guesses. He awkwardly nods his assent. "Of course, that's the most important part. And," she smiles devilishly, "the most fun. Don't you agree?" He nods again and looks away, too shy to look her in the eye. She leans forward and says, confidingly, "To tell you the truth, I just love to watch a young man shoot his load." He gasps, trembles and looks up, startled by her crudity and familiarity. And then, even more quietly, she adds, "And I know I'm going to just love watching you squirt. I bet you've got a nice big load saved up." She reaches forward and gives a quick squeeze to the hard lump that's grown in his crotch. He sighs and trembles at her sweet, tender touch on his most sensitive parts and he pushes his crotch towards her, hoping to prolong the delicious contact. "My car's over here," she says, and turns away. He follows as if in a trance.

At her apartment he notices a copy of the same issue of the campus newspaper

e notices she's drawn a happy face next to the photo of the slack sac. She notices here he's looking and says, "What a shame about those poor boys, losing their anhood. Who would do such a thing?" she asks, somewhat airily. The boy just ulps and blushes. Her casual reference to the subject turns him on: his balls tingle nd his cock starts to surge. She tells him to get undressed.

"Still," she says, appraising him coolly as he takes off his pants, "I bet it's not that ad. I bet they even enjoyed it."

"Enjoyed it!?" he exclaims, "but how...?"

"Sure," she purrs, "I think it's very possible. I bet it was something they always ecretly wanted, something very sweet and special. I bet they thanked her fterwards."

"Her?" he asks, with a quizzical sidelong look.

He finishes taking off his underpants and stands up, naked from the waist down. is cock's already hard and throbbing. He looks at her, goggle-eyed in disbelief at e things she's saying. She pointedly looks at his stiff cock and says with a sly smirk, Looks like you're pretty interested. Have you ever thought about it?" she asks. About wanting to be castrated?"

He stands mute, groping for words.

Changing the subject, she compliments him on his cleanly shaved genitals. She ays she loves how it makes him seem young, innocent and vulnerable. "Your boyish airlessness makes your hard red cock look all the more lurid and obscene."

She walks over to him, casually grasps him by his erection and leads him over to a pecial chair with a short seat and two adjustable extensions on the side to put his gs up on. Gently stroking his cock up and down she says, "I want you to do it here," nd nods at the chair.

He hesitates and she smiles, looking at him boldly, and asks, "What's the matter, ou're not worried I'm going to try and do something to you, are you?" He lowers his yes, gulps and shakes his head.

She releases his cock and then, as he gets into the chair he says quietly, almost nder his breath, "You do seem to know an awful lot about those other boys."

Ignoring him, she continues, jokingly, "And even if I did, who could blame me, ou've got such a nice pair." Smiling in his face, she bends over and reaches between is legs and gives his tight sac a soft, lingering caress. "Ummmm," she purrs, "very ice. Nice and full, round and roly-poly." He blushes and pushes his genitals towards er, automatically hoping for more of her sweet touch. He feels his whole awareness egin to descend into his bursting cock and tight, aching sac.

To his disappointment she stops touching him and goes to get another chair which she pulls right up close between his legs. As she sits down he looks at her, inquiringly, surprised that she is going to be watching while sitting so close by. She just smiles and instructs him to get down to business and start doing it.

He does as he's told and she leans forward, watching closely. Her eyes glitter an shine. "That looks like it feels so good. Does it? You look like you've done this befor Do you play with yourself a lot?" she asks, mischievously.

Beginning to descend into intense, bestial sexual abandonment, he blushes and whines, "Yes, yes I, I do, I do, I like to do it, I, I like to play with myself. I can't help it, it feels so good!" She laughs merrily at his confusion and embarrassment.

“So, tell me,” she asks, returning to her previous question, "have you ever thought about it, about wanting to surrender your manhood? To a woman?" He starts to stutter a reply but she interrupts him, "Don't be embarrassed, many men do, it's OK."

"Yes, yes, I, I..." he stammers, "I have thought about it."

"Do you fantasize about it? Is it a turn-on?" she asks. She watches him stroking himself more intensely, a drop of precum forming at the tip.

"Oh, yes, yes," he gasps, "oh yes, I like to fantasize about it, to think about what it would be like to totally surrender my manhood... to surrender it to a, a, a mean, wicked woman." He's hunched forward, his jaw slack, his eyes glazed, his hand pumping steadily.

"You're a very naughty, dirty boy, you know," she says, her voice becoming husky, her face flushed with excitement, "to fantasize about a woman taking your manhood. I wonder if that's what those other boys said before that woman took theirs."

"Oh, oh, oh, yes," he gasps, "those other boys lost, they lost their manhood. Do you really think it was a woman?"

"Oh yes," she says in a husky purr, "I'm positive. Some women love to, you know to reach right up in-between a boy's legs, tenderly open that tight, aching spot and delicately, sweetly, lovingly pluck it."

"Oh, oh, how, how do you know so much about it?" he asks. She just smiles. He continues, "I think those women are very wicked and mean. Do you, do you know any women like that?"

"Yes," she says in a low, husky whisper, "As a matter of fact I know quite a few. Would you like to meet one?"

"Yes! I mean no! I'd be too afraid to," he gasps.

"Don't be afraid, they're like me, they're very nice. When you meet one you iould just relax and open yourself to her totally, like you are now. Just trust her and t her do what she wants. When you do, it'll be very, very nice, I promise. Just like iose other boys."

"Oh, oh, are you, are you one of, one of those wicked women? Are, are you going), going to do something to me?" he cries with a mixture of hope and anguish.

"Don't be silly, it's alright. Relax. I only want you to enjoy a very sweet and)ecial experience. It'll be alright, I promise," she cooed, soothingly. "Those other)ys were very worried too, but she knew how to make them relax." Then, with a w chuckle she added, "Those poor boys. Their little empty bags looked so sad terwards."

"Oh, oh, those other boys," he gasps, "oh, oh, did they, did they enjoy it?"

"Would you like to find out for yourself? Aren't you just dying to know how it els? Would you like to meet the woman who did it?" she asks, huskily. "I can easily range it. I know she'd love to meet you."

"Yes, I'd like, I'd like to meet her, but I'm afraid. If I met her she'd, she'd take my anhood!"

"Of course she would. Especially after she saw what a nice pair you have, the mptation would be irresistible. But don't worry, it's not that bad. Just relax. I'll ke care of everything. It's very nice. You'll really like it," she says, soothingly.

He becomes tremendously inflamed and moans, "Oh, god! Oh, oh! Yes!" he cries, want her to do it! I want her to take my manhood!"

As he feels his ejaculation beginning he gets a sinking feeling when he realizes)w embarrassing it will be to perform his most private sexual function with a fully-othed woman watching. "Oh, oh, oh, I can't help it, you make me do it," he whines. ; he tenses and spreads his legs wider, getting ready to shoot, he sees her pull out pair of surgical scissors. He realizes something overwhelming and inevitable is)out to happen, something he's always secretly dreaded and also, even more cretly, wanted. "Oooooh noooooo," he whines in total, hopeless despair, "oooooh)ooooo."

She smiles devilishly up at him and says, "Time for a little snip 'n' snitch."

He shoots his first spurt and she deftly snips into his sac. Totally giving in to it, he rusts out his hips, pushing his scrotum towards her saying, "Oh yes, oh god, yes, ease, please do it, take my manhood, oh, oh, please castrate me!" He keeps roking and squirting as he watches her working between his legs. In a few

moments she finishes up and says, quietly, almost to herself, "I think I'll just take these." And then more loudly, with a low chuckle,"My, my, my, what a shameless little castration slut you turned out to be."

He has finished shooting his load and has fallen back in the chair, lost in a grogg daze, totally spent. When he hears what she said he snaps out of it and cries, "Don' How can you say that!? After what you just did! You, you took my manhood!"

"Yes, it was for your own good, and you loved it," she blithely responds. Then, with a snicker, "And your family jewels will make an excellent addition to my collection."

"You tricked me," he whines. "You planned it all along. I trusted you."

She opens a drawer and takes out some bandages and a surgical sewing kit. She begins sewing him up.

"I prefer to think of it as providing guidance," she says with a slightly offended sniff. "I merely helped you realize a special, secret dream. And believe me, it doesn take much. You dirty little boys are all alike. All you need is a little guidance and encouragement and before you know it you're spreading your legs, offering your sac, begging and squirming for me to start snipping."

He blushes furiously as he recalls how he acted.

She starts bandaging him up. "Now thank me," she says bossily.

"Th... thank you," he says, blushing and looking down at the floor.

"For what?" she demands.

"For... for... doing it," he says quietly.

"Doing what?" she says, impatiently.

"For taking my manhood!" He blurts out with an anguished yelp and then goes limp, slouching forward, his head hanging down in total resignation and defeat, staring sightlessly.

Standing over him, looking down, she says, "That's right, I took your manhood, I've done for so many. I love giving you boys what you most secretly want and need."

After a few minutes she tells him he's had time to recover and tells him to get dressed.

As she leads him to the door he looks down again at the campus newspaper an the lurid photo. She notices his glance and says, "Maybe they'll put your little emp

ag on the front page tomorrow." She laughs as he silently shuffles out the door and own the hall.

Two weeks later, while walking to class, the boy passes the woman standing on he street. She's talking to another college boy waiting at a bus stop. He sees her aise her hand and make the jerk-off gesture. Hot tears of shame and regret began o well in his eyes and he feels a sharp pang of jealousy as he watches the woman ead the other boy to her car. He also feels a twinge of pain between his legs.

. COMPANY SISSY

I've always had a big, prominent bottom, but I was surprised how much attention t got during a recent job interview at a female-run company.

After the main interview I was given a special questionnaire. The last section ontained unusually personal questions like, "when was the last time you had sex vith a partner?", "do you consider yourself primarily straight or gay?", "how many imes a day do you masturbate?", "when was the last time you masturbated?", "do ou have any sex fetishes?", and "have you ever had any submissive feelings?"

After filling out the questionnaire I was interviewed by the company doctor - a voman, of course. After looking at my questionnaire, she asked me to be more pecific about my fetishes. I blushed and stammered and timidly confessed I had a etish for being dominated by a woman. She made a note of it and smiled smugly. onsulting my questionnaire, she said I masturbated with uncommon frequency, but hat that was a good sign.

I timidly asked her how I had done and she smiled and said, "You're exactly the ort of sissy, I mean man, our company prefers. We've hired a lot of men like you nd I have a feeling you're going to fit in perfectly."

After I was started work, one of the female execs, Liza, took a special liking to me nd would often come up behind me and fondle my bottom. Each time she did it she ot more forward until she was shamelessly goosing me right up into my sensitive ole, which always gave me a highly embarrassing erection. She told me she wanted o get to know me better and invited me to her home after work. I didn't dare efuse.

Once at her home she tricked me into letting her handcuff my hands behind my ack. Then she steered me over to a high-backed chair and told me to lean over it. he unbuckled my belt and roughly pulled down my pants and bared my bottom. I imidly asked her what she was going to do but she just laughed. She complimented ne on my nice big bottom. She parted my cheeks and took a good look at my uivering, anxious hole.

I watched as she removed her skirt and panties which left her naked below the waist. I became shocked and alarmed when she strapped on a dildo which jutted ou in front of her. She asked me if my bottom had ever been penetrated. I told her it most certainly had not. She laughed and told me she loved opening up a virgin. I asked her to release me and let me go but she just laughed. As she lubed up my hol I objected strenuously. She told me to relax as she began to penetrate me. Once sh fully penetrated me she paused to lean down, reach around and jerk me off in orde to get me in the mood. To my shame and humiliation, it worked. She straightened up, grabbed hold of my hips and vigorously fucked me until I totally lost it and shot my load. She slowly pulled out and looked at my the cum running down the back of the chair. She laughed and said, "Looks like you enjoyed it after all. I think we're making good progress." Collapsed over the chair, I wept silently. I had never felt so degraded and humiliated.

On another occasion, she invited me to join her and some friends at a friend's house. There were three women and two other sissies. The other sissies also had bi bottoms like me and we were all naked. One of them, Ralph, was ordered to climb, face down, into a special chair that spread his legs and raised his ass up in a most vulnerable and accessible position. I watched with a mixture of shame and fascination as he eagerly hurried to comply. One of the women put on her strap-or stepped up behind him, penetrated him and began sodomizing him. He moaned an wiggled and shamelessly begged her to fuck him harder.

I had to admit the scene was highly arousing. The other sissy there was seated next to me and he took hold of his cock and started jerking off as we watched Ralph getting fucked. Liza gave me permission to jerk myself off too, which I shyly did at first, but was soon pumping away shamelessly. The women laughed at us and calle us naughty little sissies who can't stop playing with our little clitties. The shame just made us jerk off all the harder. They warned us not to cum because we had to save it for when it was our turn in the chair.

*** Ralph's Deflowering ***

On another occasion, Liza told me that Ralph had been quite shy before he had been "opened up", but now he craves being butt fucked. She went on to describe how, one time, they had him securely tied down in the special chair and then ushered in a fit, naked young man called Bruce who sported a sizable erection. Ralp struggled mightily to escape when he realized what they had planned. Ralph begge and pleaded with them to let him go because he knew that if he underwent what they planned it would force a change in him and there would be no turning back. The women just laughed and told him to relax and enjoy it.

Bruce started to penetrate Ralph and Ralph resisted at first but soon realized it was useless. Then Ralph relaxed and let Bruce fully penetrate him and then he lay still and silent for a few minutes while Bruce steadily fucked him, then his feelings

inally overpowered him and he shuddered and shook and began to moan with bandoned pleasure. The women all laughed and cheered when they saw that. alph's cock had also become burstingly stiff and swollen. Nonetheless, Ralph was evastated at being used for another man's sexual pleasure, especially while women vatched. When Ralph came he made a real spectacle of himself, his body stiffened nd bucked while he shot jet after jet of come on the chair underneath. Bruce came p Ralph's ass soon after, with Ralph sighing, cooing and squirming all the while. A issy always remembers receiving his first load.

After a few sessions with Bruce, Ralph really began to crave hot hard cock up his ss. This is when the women decided it was time to introduce him to fellatio. Ralph alked at first and had to be coaxed and guided, but ultimately he took Bruce's cock ully up into his mouth and sucked and licked like it was his mamma's milk. The vomen applauded when Bruce gulped down his first load.

After Liza told me this she looked at me and smiled which made me gulp and lush and look down because I realized that these things were what was in store for ne, too.

*** Promoting Big-bottomed Sissies ***

There is a glass ceiling for sissies at the company. The highest they could be romoted to is the position of personal assistant (PA) to a VP. But first he has to rove his total commitment by surrendering his manhood and submitting to astration. When Liza told me that I became very aroused. Liza noticed and smiled nd said she knew she was going to enjoy having me promoted and making me her A. The tenure of a PA lasts only one year, after which they're retired and a new issy is promoted to take their place. "After you're promoted you won't be able to lay with your little clitty anymore, you know," teased Liza. It made me sad, but the ubmissive part of me was totally giddy.

When it was time for my promotion, it was the same company doctor that had nterviewed him who performed the surgery. Liza was there, too, to witness me ffering up my manhood. "All big-bottomed sissies should be relieved of their nanhood. It only tempts them to play with their little clitties too much," said the ady doctor as she deftly started snipping into my scrotum.

After I was promoted, Liza asked me with a sly grin, "So, tell me, how do you like eing castrated?" I just blushed and hung my head while she laughed.

After I was promoted I was invited to a special party with the female execs and neir PA's. The PA's had to wait on the execs, serving food and drinks. The PA's wore othing but short, open vests and slippers. Their nipples and rubbery little clitties vere both painted a bright red. This lewd display of so many castrated sissies gave ne women much delight throughout the evening.

During the evening, one of the women would occasionally stop one of the sissies play with his little peeny and ask him how he liked being castrated and he always answered that he was very happy and grateful. Then she would ask him if he ever missed being able to play with himself. He always answered that he did, a little. The she would coo soothingly and play with his little, rubbery, bright-red clittty. This would cause his little clitty to swell and stiffen as he whimpered with pleasure, but that was all he could do.

7. CONSULATATION WITH A CASTRATRIX

"Only in San Francisco," I thought to myself, "could you find five offices in the same block, each one openly advertising the services of a castratrix." I chose the one with the humorous shingle: the image of a large, pendulous scrotum and a pair of stainless steel scissors open and poised to close on the neck of the scrotum. A lady' elegant, manicured hand is shown wielding the scissors. Embossed on the shingle are the words "Ms. Veronika van Gelder, Certified Castratrix".

The waiting room is half full of nervous, fidgety men, some alone, some with their wives or girlfriends.

After waiting 45 minutes, my name is called and I am shown into a small office.

Ms. van Gelder is in her early thirties and is very attractive and very confident. She sits behind her desk and looks at me with a sly smirk and a twinkle in her eyes.

"And why have you come to see us today, Mr. Jones?"

"Oh, just for an exam. I'm just curious, you know, I just wanted to find out what would be involved."

"Yes, of course, that's what all my patients say on their first visit."

She gives me a form to sign. I read the form and one sentence catches my eye.

"I, the undersigned do hereby consent to be examined by the above named Certified Castratrix, and further, I agree to meekly submit to any and all additional procedures that are verbally consented to during the course of the examination."

I ask Ms. van Gelder to expain what the sentence means.

She smiles again and purrs "Oh, that's just a catch-all clause. We've found that it saves alot of time and paper work. Quite frequently, things come up during the course of an exam that are best dealt with without delay."

Before I can ask her what sort of things she is referring to, Ms. van Gelder tells me to go through a door to her exam room.

Waiting in the exam room are two lovely young girls in nurses uniforms. Ms. van elder introduces them to me: Nurse Elaine and Nurse Maryann.

Ms. van Gelder tells me to strip and lie on the exam table with my feet in the irrups.

I do as I am told and I quickly develop an erection as I lie naked and exposed on ie exam table in front of these three sexy young women.

Ms. van Gelder steps between my legs and immediately starts handling and queezing my scrotum.

"Yes, Mr. Jones, you seem to have a good pair of balls in your sac. But they're eally quite hairy, aren't they? I'm afraid I'm going to have to shave you down there, Ir. Jones, in order to conduct a thorough and complete exam."

Ms. van Gelder applies some shaving cream to my tight scrotum. My bursting ecker starts to drool while she is shaving me. She notices this and tells Nurse Elaine start milking me. I sigh and moan as I feel Nurse Elaine's soft fingers curl around y throbbing cock and begin slowing stroking me.

After Ms. van Gelder is done shaving me, she wipes the leftover shaving cream ff with a warm, wet cloth. When she sees my naked, pink, hairless scrotum, she queals with delight.

"Oh, I just love the sight of a freshly shaved scrotum! Just look, girls, isn't it just dorable!"

Ms. van Gelder begins to excitedly tickle and squeeze and pluck at my balls in eir wrinkly sac.

"Oh, yes, Mr. Jones, you've got a splendid pair of balls! I'm so glad you decided to sit us today so I could see them and handle them."

This leaves me totally flustered, but finally I manage to ask, "Could you tell me ease, what would be involved in the procedure, Ms. van Gelder?"

"Well, it's really very simple, Mr. Jones. First, just a slight pinprick while I inject u with local anesthetic."

Ms. van Gelder snaps her fingers and holds out her hand, Nurse Maryann hands er a hypodermic needle. Ms. van Gelder quickly jabs the hypo into me near my ball c, and starts depressing the plunger.

I wince and asks her what she's doing.

"Oh, nothing, Mr. Jones. I noticed just now that you seemed to have some extra nsitivity down in your groin area, so I thought it best to alleviate it."

"Oh, good, I thought for a moment that maybe you might be getting me ready for..."

"Ready for what, Mr. Jones?"

"Oh, you know, I thought you might be getting me ready to do that thing to me, you know, that thing we were talking about."

"Oh, you mean that procedure I'm certified to perform?"

"Yes, yes, that's the one I mean."

"Why that's silly, Mr. Jones, I couldn't do that. Not without obtaining your consent first, I couldn't."

Ms. van Gelder asks Nurse Elaine how the milking is coming. "Oh, I think he's about ready", she replies.

"Good, good, then why don't you go ahead and finish milking him while we watch."

Ms. van Gelder and Nurse Maryann watch, giggling and smirking slyly, as Nurse Elaine firmly, but sweetly, milks my bursting cock. Soon I loose control to the bursting feeling between my legs and start to grunt and squirt thick hot globs of cu onto my hairy belly. After I am done squirting, Ms. van Gelder tells me what a gooc boy I am, and thanks me for giving them such a sexy show. Then she tells Nurse Elaine to clean me up.

After I've recovered from my intense ejaculation, I ask, "How many men have y seen today, Ms. van Gelder, if you don't mind my asking?"

"No, no, I don't mind. Four. I've seen four. Each one told me he just wanted an exam, just like you, Mr. Jones. But once I got them up on my exam table, it was eas to get them to admit that they were secretly aching for me to give them much mor than a simple exam."

"You don't mean..."

"Mean what, Mr. Jones?"

"You don't mean to tell me that you actually went ahead and did that, you kno that thing to them..."

"Why yes, Mr. Jones, yes, that is exactly what I did do to them, as it so happens And they thanked me for it afterwards. Oh, don't looked so shocked, Mr. Jones. It really wasn't very hard for me to persuade them to finally admit the real reason th had came to visit me in my office, and what it really was they wanted me to do to them. And, unless I'm very much mistaken, I suspect that you've been hiding a littl

ecret from me as well, haven't you, Mr. Jones?"

She was leaning over me and smiling knowingly, expectantly. She kept my crotum gently cupped in the palm of her hand, but I had lost all feeling in it.

I looked up at her, gulped, and then said, "What do you mean, Ms. van Gelder. Vhat secret do you think I'm hiding from you?"

"You know very well what I'm referring to, Mr. Jones. And I think it's time you topped fooling yourself and admitted the real reason you came to my office today. 'mon, tell us, we're waiting."

I gulped again and whispered that I was secretly dying to be castrated.

"Is there anything else you'd like to tell us, Mr. Jones?"

"Yes, I want, I want to be castrated, and I want, I want you, Ms. van Gelder, I vant you to do it to me, please, please, please, Ms. van Gelder, please castrate me! lease!" I pushed myself a couple inches down the table, pressing my scrotum into er hand, wriggling and squirming it against her palm.

"Excellent, excellent," said Ms. van Gelder, smiling smugly and squeezing and lucking at my profferred scrotum, "that's more like it." She nodded to Nurse Aaryann, who handed her a scalpel.

"Why, it'll be my pleasure to help you with that request, Mr. Jones, it'll be my leasure." She laughed softly to herself. "I had a feeling it wouldn't take long for you o give me your consent."

I felt a slight pressure as Ms. van Gelder began to make a small incision in the left ide of my scrotum. Her assistants began to giggle.

. DOWN ON THE FARM WITH MS. VAN GELDER

ummary: The Bay Area's busiest Castratrix takes a well earned rest upstate at her ural farm.

Ms. Veronica Van Gelder leans back in the driver's seat as she heads upstate in er black Lexus Infiniti (with all the options) for a two week getaway at her secluded ural farm. It would not be an exaggeration to say she's well off.

She heaves a long sigh of exhaustion. She has definitely been experiencing the ownside of being the Bay Area's hardest working Certified Public Castratrix. She as over-worked. She'd been spreading herself way too thin. In addition to her busy

practice she had also taken on jobs as consultant to a number of local area organizations.

She was a consultant to a local organization of professional dominatrixes and to local group of human-horse/pony-play enthusiasts and to a local chain of kinky fetis bookstores and boutiques.

She was also a special, honorary member of a sizable association of eunuchs. Sh was always thrilled to attend their annual banquet where she and a number of othe castratrixes were honored guests. She found the company of eunuchs to be very sweet and agreeable in general and she also loved meeting again the ones she'd personally castrated. In fact, there was a ritual at the end of each banquet where th castratrixes would sit in a row, a few feet apart, at the back of the room while a dozen or so eunuchs lined up in front of each. As each eunuch came to the front of the line he would take down his pants, spread his legs and thrust his crotch forward offering himself for inspection. The castratrix would gently reach between his legs and feel around.

"My, my," she would say, quietly, "I can't seem to find your balls. What happene to them?"

"They're... they're... they're gone," the eunuch would say with a gulp. "I was castrated."

"You were?" she would say, with a sly smile. "Who did it to you?"

"It... it was... you, you did it, you did it to me," the eunuch would say.

"And how do you feel about that?" she would coyly ask.

"I... I... I want to thank you, thank you for... for... for castrating me!" he would gasp.

"Of course," she would purr, "you're very welcome. Believe me, it was my pleasure."

Then he would pull up his pants and leave the line and the next eunuch would step up and pull down his pants.

Ms. Van Gelder was also consultant to a small eunuch prostitution ring run by a couple of hard-ass bull dykes. Some men, and a few women, found special delight i enjoying the sexual favors of eunuchs. And some clients were always eager to enjoy new, cherry, or fresh-cut, ones, and it was up to Ms. Van Gelder to perform the necessary alteration. She did feel a little bad about how these meek little eunuchs were dominated and exploited. She also had heard that cunnilingus received from such a eunuch was a rare delight but had yet to sample it.

She was also a special contributor to an annual, private, by invitation only, veekend-long TestyFesty, or testicle festival. Her special contribution was, along vith a few other local area castratrixes, bags of frozen testicles that she had ccumulated during the year. The TestyFesty was organized by a small group of ominant women and it was attended primarily by their female friends and ubmissives. It centered around a banquet where fried testicles were the main ourse, but there were also a few other events and activities. She'd heard it was a un weekend but had yet to make a point of attending.

She was also consultant to the kinky fetish magazine, Castratrix Quarterly. ecently she was the consultant on the filming of a Castratrix Quarterly produced ideo about two evil dominatrixes who trick a hapless dweeb into allowing himself o be tied up with his scrotum held securely in a small, but very sharp, guillotine. It vas her job to clean him up after they pulled the release cord and neatly sliced him. f course, the actor that volunteered for the part didn't realize he was really going o be cut.

She was also consultant to the big, annual kinky fetish ball. All of the groups nentioned above supported it and took part. The highlight was a contest between 5 male submissives, the winner of which was to lose his nutsack. The contest took lace in front of a large audience. The submissives were strapped naked in a bent-ver forward posture to bondage frames. Naked dominatrixes with dildoes strapped their hips stood behind them, gripping their hips and vigorously sodomizing them. ach contestant's genitals was spotlighted and displayed up on a big screen so veryone in the audience could see. The first one to lose control and cum was the vinner. A raffle was given in connection with the contest where the prize to be won vas the nutsack-change-purse and testicle-earrings set resulting from the contest. he raffle was open to dominant women only, of course.

She was also a consultant to the local area high schools. Recently she was called to help deal with a teen that was getting erections all the time during school ours, shamelessly playing pocket pool during class, even occasionally exposing imself to the female staff and students, most notably to the cheer-leading squad. As. Van Gelder was more than happy to help them nip his problem in the bud, so to peak. After that he became the laughingstock of the school. They even forced him wear a t-shirt for a week that had the word "Eunuch" printed on the front and ack.

Ms. Van Gelder was so over-worked and over-extended that she was seeing crotums and testicles coming at her relentlessly in her dreams at night.

She was also depressed by how common and mainstream castration was ecoming. Recent issues of both Cosmopolitan and Esquire had run articles amorizing and promoting it. It was losing its edge. She was considering changing er profession.

She snaps out of her funk as she arrives at her farm. She goes in the main house and discovers a cabinet open that should have been locked and some of the issues of Castratrix Quarterly she kept there missing. She suspects her handsome young handyman and caretaker, Joe.

Quietly fuming, she stalks out to the barn. She finds Joe sitting on a bale of hay, facing a three-quarter turn away from her, naked except for a t-shirt. His right hand obviously busy in his lap, his right elbow jiggling rhythmically. His left hand holds a magazine. She creeps up from behind. She sees the magazine is Castratrix Quarterly He's reading the three page cartoon story, "Human horse", that's at the end of each issue. The formula for each episode of this story is always the same. The human horse tries, and narrowly succeeds, in eluding various combinations of dominant women who are eager to capture and geld him. At the end, when he finally thinks he's out of the woods and can relax he finds he's fallen into a clever trap and he loses his freedom and his balls all in one fell swoop. In the final panel of the story th dominant women gloat and grin wickedly in triumph while the human gelding hang his head in total humiliation and resignation. It's at this last sequence in the story that Joe is jerking off to. She waits until he shoots his load. Totally spent, he lets the magazine drop to the ground.

"Enjoying yourself?" she asks, dryly.

Twisting around quickly to face her, he blurts, "Ms. Van Gelder! I... I..." He lunge to cover his crotch with his hands.

"You are, of course, aware of what I do for a living?" she asks, coldly.

"Yes, Ms. Van Gelder. But I... I..." he stammers.

"Get dressed and come see me in the house in half an hour," she says.

"You're not going to... going to...?" he asks, worriedly.

"Castrate you? I never castrate a male until he's ready. Just do as I say," she says

When he comes in she tells him he'll have to be punished. But first she gives him a couple hours of chores to do and tells him to come see her in the house when he' done.

Two hours later he comes back to see her, sweaty and tired. He finds her sitting in her living room, naked except for a strap-on dildo. She gives him a Fleet enema k and tells him to give himself an enema. Afterwards she leads him out to the barn and tells him to strip and get down into the gelding stocks and straps him into them She proceeds to sodomize him until he cums. She pulls out and looks down in smug satisfaction at his limp, spent body hanging weakly in the stocks. His butthole is stil twitching and quivering. She gently prods it with her index and middle finger. He trembles, sighs and moans submissively, totally giving himself up to the feelings

's stirring in him. She laughs quietly. She pushes her fingers in an inch into his ping, well-lubricated butthole and gently finger fucks him. He pants, gasps, ggles and pushes his ass back to encourage her casual, playful penetration. She ghs a loud, deep-throated laugh. He's so obviously putty in her dominant hands.

She stops playing with his ass and lets him out of the stocks. She tells him that in tack room there's a bridle, bit, reins and harness for a human horse and tells him go fetch them. While he's gone she takes off the strap-on and puts on a t-shirt d jogging shorts. He returns with the gear and she puts it on him. She takes him to the paddock behind the barn and puts him through his paces as a human rse for the first time. He soon becomes hotly erect during this play. She leads him ck inside the barn. As he stands there with all his human horse gear on she comes close to him, putting her left arm around his waist and pressing the left side of soft, fragrant body against him. She grasps his hard cock with her right hand and wly strokes. "Of course you realize, don't you," she says softly, "if you're going to my human horse you're also going to have to be gelded."

When he hears that he gasps, grunts and blurts, "Oh, oh, oh, Ms. Van Gelder! I n't help it! You make me do it!" And he thrusts his hips forward, spurting again d again. She watches and chuckles, gently stroking his still-pulsing organ.

DREAM FULFILLMENT

stration has always been my strongest sex fetish. One day I decided to have it ne for real.

I get a referral for a lifestyle castratrix from a 'kink friendly' lady psychologist.

We meet up. She's an attractive and very confident woman in her early 40s.

She tells me she loves to dominate and that castration is the ultimate pleasure d fulfillment, to surgically penetrate a male and to take his maleness and his sex nction from him.

She tells me she doesn't castrate strangers. She has to get to know a male before e castrates. She needs to take a strong personal interest.

I spend several months being her domestic slave and general submissive before e deems it is time.

Late one night, we go to a quiet, unoccupied obstetrics clinic lent to her by an stetrician lady friend.

I'm nervous at first but soon get into the mood to totally offer myself to her.

Afterwards, I continue to serve as her submissive. She openly gloats and teases me about my eunuch status. She shows me off to her friends as her latest eunuch. After a couple months she finds a new submissive and I'm no longer needed. She gives me away to a lady friend that enjoys having eunuch servants.

10. ERIC'S CORRECTION

Sandra Jones is fed up with her husband Eric's bad attitude and disobedience so she decides to take him to her friend Julia's correction center that offers a guaranteed remedy for poorly performing husbands.

On the appointed day, Julia's all-female correction center staff are all smiles when they greet Sandra and Eric. Their smiling faces are extra-bright because they all share a special, naughty secret about what's about to happen.

Leaving Sandra in the waiting room, Julia escorts Eric into her exam room. Her two young female assistants are already there, waiting.

Julia tells him she's going to begin with a simple physical exam. She orders him strip and get up onto her exam table.

They position him on the table so that his feet are up in the stirrups, his knees are up in the air, spread wide apart and his butt is lying squarely on the front edge the table. This results in leaving the area between his legs totally open and vulnerable.

The assistants quickly move to strap him down securely to the table.

With a warm smile Julia steps between his legs and begins shaving his scrotum.

Eric: With a slightly shaky voice, he asks her what she's doing.

Julia: I'm just going to perform a simple little procedure on your little sex glands

Eric: "My... my sex glands?" his voice getting tense and shaky. "Does, does... my wife know about... about this??"

Julia: Oh yes, in fact she specifically requested it. And it's perfectly normal, I perform it on all the males that visit my correction center. It invariably results in a great improvement in their attitude. You'll have a lot more respect for your wife after this, Mr. Jones. And a lot more respect for women in general.

Eric: Is it... is it like a vasectomy?

Julia: "Why yes, it is similar," she says with a smile. "And you certainly won't be producing any more sperm from now on," she laughs, as she continues working

etween his legs.

Eric: "Oh no!" he suddenly cries. "Oh no, stop! Please, I beg you, don't do it!)on't do this to me!"

Julia: "Ha ha," she laughs, "this is my favorite part of the procedure, when the nale finally realizes what's happening."

Eric: "Please, please, please, don't do it!" he cries piteously.

Julia: I'm very sorry, Mr. Jones, but it's much too late. I'm almost done. I just have o put a few more stitches in your scrotum and you'll be ready to go.

In the waiting room on the way out:

Julia: Everything went very well, Mrs. Jones. I think you'll be very pleased with he results.

As they leave, Julia thinks to herself: We all love watching a man leaving the enter, knowing what's been done, knowing the small but all-important change hat's been done to him.

In the car on the way home:

Eric: Do you know what they did to me??

Sandra: Of course, Eric. But don't fuss, it was for you own good. Life is going to be lot less stressful from now on.

Some weeks later in the living room of the Jones residence, Eric is serving Sandra nd her friend Rachel drinks and hors d'oeuvres.

Rachel: Eric seems to have a lot nicer attitude lately.

Sandra: Oh yes, he is much improved since I took him over to Julia's correction enter.

Rachel: Oh, you don't mean...?

Sandra: Yes, I decided it was high time to 'fix' his little attitude problem and put im in his place once and for all. And with such a simple solution so close at hand iere was really no reason not to. And in all fairness, I did warn him that something ke this might happen.

Rachel: How is he handling the transition?

Sandra: Well, it was a great shock at first but he's mostly gotten over it. He still gets moody from time to time. What he misses the most is not being able to play with his little peeny anymore. You know how men love to play with themselves.

Rachel: Oh yes, I know exactly what you mean. My Howie is always doing it.

Rachel: After a pause, "Can we talk to him about it?"

Sandra: Why certainly. Eric, tell Rachel what you are now.

Eric: "I... I'm a... I'm a eunuch," he says, blushing and hanging his head in shame.

Sandra: "And what is a eunuch, Eric?" she asks, smiling quietly.

Eric: "It's a man... a man that's been... castrated!" he answers, ending in an anguished little squeak.

The two women look at each other and smile.

11. FEMALE-LED MARRIAGE

One afternoon, Emily and Marge were sharing a glass of wine in Emily's spacious sunlit living room.

Emily: "Did I ever tell you how my husband lost his testicles?"

Marge: "No, not really. How did it happen?"

Emily: "Well, when I proposed to Jim I made it very clear that I'd be wearing the pants in the family. After a few months, as I half-expected, he began to be stubborn and assertive. Finally, I warned him if things didn't change I'd take certain steps. Actually, I'd already made an appointment with a special doctor."

"Oh dear", murmured Marge.

Emily: "The doctor told him she specialized in treating troubled marriages. His behavior showed he needed help coping with his manhood. 'In other words,' she said, 'you need me to take your testicles, don't you?'"

Emily: "In a shaky voice he agreed. Then she told him he needed to say, 'Please castrate me', which he did. I glowed with satisfaction when I heard that."

Emily: "He cried and whimpered as she did the work."

Marge: "And how does he feel now?"

Emily: "Well, he has definitely learned who's boss."

Marge: "I see. And where is he now?"

Emily: "Oh, Jim's in the kitchen getting ready for some company coming over. It's two or three of his eunuch friends."

Marge: "Interesting. And how did Jim's friends lose their testicles?"

Emily: "The same way. Well, Robbie was different, he jerked off too much."

Marge: "What do they do? Socialize?"

Emily: "That's right. Just talk over everyday things, mostly problems pleasing their wives."

Marge: "Do they ever talk about... being neutered?"

Emily: "No, except when their wives use it to punish them."

Marge: "Punish? How?"

Emily: "Well, to shame them, you know, their wives will remind them they're no longer a man. To make it worse, they say it in front of other people."

Marge: "Oh, my goodness! How awful."

Emily: "It's very effective. Their wives rarely have to use physical punishment."

Marge: After a pause, "And what about sex?"

Emily: "Well, Jim is very good at giving oral, most eunuchs are. You should try it yourself, Marge."

Marge: "Oh my! Why, I, I suppose maybe..."

Emily: "As for full sex, I have a couple boyfriends. Quite good ones, too."

Marge: "And they come here, to your home?"

Emily: "Why, of course! I even let Jim watch if he's been good. His little peeny gets so stiff, ha ha!"

Marge: "He doesn't sleep with you, I suppose."

Emily: "Oh no. He has a nice little cot set up in the storage room in back."

Marge: "You said eunuchs give good oral. How many have you known?"

Emily: "Quite a few. I belong to a local eunuch-swapping group. Plus, Jim isn't my

first neutered hubby."

Marge: "Wow! Was Jim aware of that when you proposed?"

Emily: "Absolutely, I was completely frank. It just made him more devoted. Men like Jim are fascinated by it."

Marge: "No wonder he didn't resist it."

Emily: "Right." After a pause, "Well, just say the word, Marge, and you can sample Jim's oral skills, ha ha!"

Marge, flustered and giddy: "Oh my! Oh! Oh!"

Both women laugh happily.

12. FIXING LITTLE JIMMY

Little Jimmy lives with his attractive, divorced mother and his sexy older sister i a small house in suburbia. Little Jimmy earned his nickname by being an immature, whiny little mamma's boy.

Max, their little pet dog, has begun masturbating frequently so the mother decides to have him fixed.

Coincidentally, Little Jimmy has just turned 18 and has also begun playing with himself a lot, and quite openly, too. The mother tells him to come along with her tc the vet.

At the vet, the mother hands Max over to a young female assistant and takes Little Jimmy in to see the sexy lady vet.

The mother tells the vet about Max's masturbation problem and the vet smiles and said she'd be happy to fix that. Then the mother tells the vet about Little Jimmy's similar problem. Little Jimmy whines and says she is embarrassing him. She tells him to shush. The vet is very sympathetic.

"And we're always catching him at it," the mother complains. "Just last week or of my daughter's girlfriends caught him doing it on the toilet. He cried out, 'Oh, oh, look at me!' and then squirted!"

They both laugh, but then the vet scowls and says, "But really, how awful."

Then the mother goes on, "And we're always been finding little puddles and smears of his smelly cum all over the house. Really, I'm at my wit's end."

The vet thinks for a moment and then says, "Well, one way to fix it is to do the

me to thing to Jimmy as to Max."

"Really?" asks the mother. "Is that possible?"

"Oh, yes," smiles the vet, "it's very possible. It's not something I do every day but ou wouldn't be the first mom that's asked for help with this."

"But they were all 18, right?" asks the mother.

"Oh yes!" exclaims the vet. "I wouldn't dream of doing anything remotely sexual ith someone under the age of 18.

Little Jimmy is listening intently now.

"But to get back to your first question," the vet continues, "I even had one oman who brought in her husband!"

"Oh my goodness!" exclaims the mother. "What did you do?"

"Well," says the vet with a twinkle, "let's just say he was a much better husband hen he left the clinic that day!" They both laugh.

"I wish I'd thought of that before I got my divorce," says the mother and they oth laugh again.

"But seriously," continues the mother, "how could you get a man to let you do at?"

"Oh, it was really pretty easy," the vet replies, "he thought he was just going to njoy a kinky little sex scene. He said he always wondered what it would be like to e fixed. But he was just so sweet the way he spread his legs and offered himself, I st couldn't resist. He had such a sweet, tight little sac!"

"And then it turned out to be the real thing?" suggests the mother.

"Well, it was certainly a whole lot kinkier than he expected," says the vet with a uiet smile.

There is silence for a few moments while the mother tries to absorb what she's st heard. Then she asks, "Could you tell me what would be involved?"

"Of course," says the vet. "In fact, I can even give you a little walk-through."

The vet tells Jimmy to strip off his pants and underpants and climb onto her ble. He gets an erection which makes the women laugh. "He probably wants to ay with himself right now," says the mother. "Isn't that right, Little Jimmy?"

Little Jimmy whines and nods and says, "Yes, can I... can I, please...?"

"Of course not!" snaps the mother indignantly.

A little bead of precum forms on the tip of his erection.

The vet describes the operation. "First we shave him, then we inject the anesthetic." Then she gently touches the spots on his tight little scrotum showing where she will make the incisions. His erection bobs and starts to drool. She tells how she will squeeze out his balls and snip his cords.

"Oh, his scrotum is just so sweet and tight!" exclaims the vet. "I'd love to open him up right now!" She offers to call in her assistant and do it for free right then an there.

Precum drools out and makes a small puddle on his abdomen. Little Jimmy is frightened but also very excited and he has to fight the urge to grab it and jerk off.

The mother tells the vet she's very tempted. She says Little Jimmy would look very cute with an empty little sac.

Little Jimmy is terrified. "No! No! Please! I promise to be good! Please don't!" Suddenly, he squeezes his eyes shut and cries out, "Oh! Oh! I can't help it!" and starts humping the air and ejaculating.

The women watch in stunned silence. Then the vet hands him some tissues and the mother says, "Ugh! Disgusting! How could you?!" Little Jimmy just squirms and whimpers.

Little Jimmy gets dressed and they go out to the waiting room and wait for the vet to get done with Max.

As they're leaving, the vet says to the mother, "I love my work, especially the castrations. Please feel free to bring Little Jimmy in any time. I'll be glad to take of him for you." Little Jimmy whimpers and the two women exchange a quiet glance and a soft smile.

As soon as they get home Little Jimmy rushes to his bedroom to urgently jerk himself off. The mother smiles knowingly.

13. GOOD LITTLE PIGGY

[Note: All characters are of legal age to engage in sexual activities]

Aunt Abigail is a handsome, fleshy brunette in her early forties. She's wearing jeans and a work shirt that's tied up high under her big tits like a halter top.

Young Tommy is a slim, blond teen. He's dressed in shorts and a t-shirt.

She circles the stocks, deftly strapping him in.

She lubes his bottom hole and tells him to relax while she inserts a butt plug. He gasps as it pops into place.

Standing up straight and tall, she looks down on him, her hands on her hips, smiling broadly. "Oh, what a sweet little piggy I have here today! It's been so long since I last had one in my stocks."

She sits down on a milking stool beside him. She unties her shirt and lets her big tits swing free. Her big, pink nipples stand out stiff and erect. She reaches behind him and flicks on the vibrating butt plug.

"Oh, Aunt Abigail!" he exclaims, overcome by the vibrating sensations in his bottom.

"Call me momma, Tommy," she instructs. She leans forward, her stiff nipples brushing against him, and reaches between his legs. "My goodness!" she exclaims. "What a dirty, naughty little piggy! Just look at how hard your little front piggy tail i And there's so much piggy-slime drooling from the tip!"

"Oh, momma!" gasps Tommy, "I... I... I can't help it!"

"Well then, I better see about milking all that dirty piggy slime right out of it," sh says in a playful, childish voice.

She starts milking him. He gasps and moans and strains in his bonds.

"I bet you're like all the other little piggy boys, I bet you're always sneaking around to find secret places so you can play with your naughty front piggy tail," she says.

He blushes deeply and quietly gasps, "Oh, oh, oh yes, momma."

She starts gently milking him. He sighs with pleasure. "I know all about you naughty little piggy boys. I bet you play with your dirty little piggy tail until you squi your piggy slime."

He blushes again, but all he can say is, "Oh momma! Oh! Oh! Oh!"

After a while, he asks, "Those other boys, did you... did you... ?"

"Yes, I gelded them", she says casually. "You can meet some of them later".

"And... and... are you... are you gonna... ?" he asks anxiously.

"Of course, my dear little piggy," she softly purrs, still stroking him. "Big momm always makes her little piggies squeal. And you want me to, don't you?"

"Oh yes!" he gasps, "Please!" Then he lets out a strangled cry and begins quirting his slime. She chuckles.

She wipes her milking hand clean on a rag and reaches behind him to turn off the utt plug. Then she stands up, moves the stool behind him and sits down.

"OK little piggy, time for you to give yourself to big momma," she says quietly.

"Oh momma!" he cries out.

He feels her snipping into his tender pouch. He begins to squeal.

"Good little piggy," she says with a chuckle.

4. HOUSE HUSBAND

I'm a successful business woman. I wanted a house husband I could depend on to o the cooking and housekeeping chores. So I went 'shopping' for one.

Males have a lot of silly ideas about taking the lead in a relationship. They want ɔ be the 'breadwinner' and to 'bring home the bacon'. I knew I'd have to work to ɿold my new husband into the role I planned and to make him accept his place.

Having a house husband is not as unusual as it used to be. Many women have ɿem. Unfortunately, their recent popularity has made it difficult to acquire one. Many males have heard that becoming a house husband is a permanent choice.

I knew Howie was submissive when I met him. I brought him home on our first ate and immediately took charge. I made him admit he was a virgin and that his nly sexual relief came from jerking off. Admitting this made him blush and fluster.

Then I told him I wanted to see his penis. As I expected, he found my domination rousing and he showed me a stiff erection. Although intensely embarrassing, all ssies love to show their little peeny to a woman like me. We both knew what was ɔming next. I told him to show me how he jerks off. Being made to do this is deeply umiliating for males. Their most private sexual function is treated as an amusing laything.

This became a regular part of our dates. I soon introduced other humiliating ctivities such as cunnilingus, analingus and sodomizing him with a strap-on. I also njoyed spanking him for minor infractions. I found his almost-frantic reaction to eing figged to be especially amusing. Whatever it was, he always meekly ubmitted.

To further cement my dominance I included other people in our sessions. I put im through his paces in front of some of my lady friends, which he found

devastating. I also made him give oral service to my lady friends while the rest of us watched, sipped martinis and commented. I brought in gay men and let them use him. My goal was to completely erode his masculinity. He lost all interest in his career and came to live only for these sessions. He was distressed when he couldn't see me regularly.

When I brought up the topic of house husband he became very quiet. He knew what it meant. He loved the idea of living in my home and seeing me every day but he knew that once he accepted there was no turning back.

I spoke soothingly to him and assured him that he would soon get used to it and that he wouldn't be lonely because he’d be able to socialize with other house husbands.

We were married soon after in a simple ceremony. He quit his job and came to live full-time in my large, modern house.

After a few months, as I expected, he began to show an independent streak. He also became needy about our sex sessions and I caught him masturbating a few times without permission. I realized the time had come for the final adjustment.

We both knew that this was inevitable. He was saddened and apprehensive but he didn't resist when I drove him to the clinic. Afterwards, the clinic ladies told me he’d been very good and had been eager for the lady surgeon to begin.

After a few months all his behavioral problems were resolved and he became th completely docile and obedient husband I’d wanted all along.

Now, whenever we let the husbands get together one of the things they talk about is how big their peenies used to get and how much they enjoyed playing with them. Of course, now their peenies are very small and can never get hard. It’s a litt sad we had to take that away from them but it’s the only way to put them in their place.

My lady friends and I occasionally like to stage a private contest. The contest is see which husband has the smallest peeny. We make them dye their peenies and nipples red and then parade around naked while we watch and compare.

15. JAKE GETS CLIPPED

Jake was a human pony-boy on Samantha's ranch. It was a medium sized ranch stocked with many other, similar pony-boys. Samantha had searched all over the world to gather together the prize pony-boys she kept at her ranch. Also, since her ranch was located in a region with a hot climate, her ponies were always kept buck naked.

Samantha would often take one of her ponies out and harness him to a small, vo-wheeled buggy and have him pull her around in it at a slow canter while she ghtly whipped his sweating, straining flanks.

She often sponsored special weekends when she would invite over a group of her dy friends. It was customary on such weekends for her to stage a race between erself and a half dozen of her friends with each one driving a buggy being pulled by sweating, panting pony-boy.

Samantha was especially fond of geldings. Some of her ponies were geldings hen they first came to her ranch, but others had been gelded after. She always ept the health and happiness of her ponies foremost, however, so when it came me to have one of her ponies gelded, she always made sure to have it done in the ost medically safe, and painless way possible. One of her best friends was a lady et who knew just how to do it, and who had carried it out on human males many nes, and who greatly enjoyed and savored performing the task. Samantha herself ok special delight in watching and helping out during these procedures.

Samantha's domination and control over her ponies was complete. Whenever e wanted sex she always choose a gelding to serve her. She was very fond of cieving oral tribute. She would recline on a large overstuffed sofa in the stable and ke her loose skirt up above her waist until her hot, musky, bushy sex was fully posed and accessible.

She would spread her firm, creamy thighs wide apart and call the lucky gelding er to her. He would stand next to her while she reached up between his legs and isurely fingered his loose, empty sac.

Then she would give him the signal to get down on his knees between her legs d start licking and lapping at her soft, warm, moist pussy lips. Soon, his whole face ould be buried in her throbbing wetness as she pressed down on the back of his ad, pushing him harder and deeper into her center of pleasure.

On those weekends that she threw parties, she encouraged each of her refined d discriminating lady friends to bring a eunuch of their own. After a day of gorous outdoor activities, there would be a sumptuous dinner indoors, followed by very pleasant cocktail hour, whereupon the room would be filled with the sounds tinkling ice cubes, hearty, easy laughter, and occasional girlish giggles punctuating e ladies' conversations. Their eunuchs would stand quietly and respectfully at their des. The servants, of course, were all castrated males who wore skimpy, crotchless iforms that plainly revealed for all to see the manner in which they had been ered.

After cocktails, it was customary for the women to retire to a large room rnished only with many large cushions. Once there, they and their eunuch dates ould disrobe and then the ladies would proceed to use their dates to satisfy their

own sexual pleasure. Oral tribute from the eunuchs, and strap-on dildo penetratio of them, were the ladies' two favorite methods of deriving sexual gratification fron their eunuchs. Samantha, their most gracious host, was very fond of giving her eunuchs a good hard fucking up the ass with a strap-on. She was often heard to remark at these get-togethers that there was nothing on earth to compare with th thrill of giving a eunuch's ass a good hard workout with a strap-on.

As a warm-up to these eunuch orgies, Samantha would often provide stimulatir entertainment.

For example, she would arrange to have one of the uncut ponies sit up on a raised platform and put on a show for them with his hard cock. All the ladies woulc watch in hushed anticipation, with bright eyes and wide grins as he would slowly stroke his purple, drooling prick. Hearty belly laughs, and delighted squeals would erupt from the women when he climaxed and his throbbing, bursting penis would spew out thick, sloppy squirts. And, as the last drops oozed out of the uncut male's drooping pecker, Samantha, with a merry twinkle in her eye, would loudly announ to one and all that the star of the show was scheduled to be castrated the followin week. Seeing the look of shock and dismay on the uncut male's face as he heard th news always drew a big, hearty laugh from the ladies.

Watching a pony actually being gelded was another favorite entertainment for the guests at these parties.

It wasn't a universally popular entertainment, however, since there were alway a few women that were squeamish at the sight of blood.

Jake had been a pony on the ranch for six months and he was one of Samantha favorites. She liked him so much that she had let him give her oral tributes on a number of occasions, and had given his ass a number of vigorous workouts with he sturdy strap-on. And the thing that was so incredibly exceptional about this was th his balls were still intact!

Jake was really a very foolish pony though, because he thought that since he ha been given these exceptional privileges, that this meant he would also be spared from joining the ranks of his gelded comrades. But also, deep in his heart, he secretly yearned to give himself completely to his adored owner and give up his manhood for her. Samantha was wise and patient and let Jake enjoy his few days a her ranch as a throbbing, spurting, uncut male. But one day, when she and her lad Vet friend came into the stable, Jake knew the time had come for him to be led, meekly and submissively to Samantha's Castration Corral!

The next day was bright and warm and sunny, and Jake felt a little twinge of pa between his legs. But he felt warm and happy, because Samantha had come out to the stable to softly, and lovingly pet him and murmur to him and give him a little k on the cheek and tell him she was so proud of him starting out on this first day of

ew life.

6. KINKY FETISH BOUTIQUE

Summary: Nerdy little castration freak stumbles onto magazine of his wildest reams, and then gets more than he bargained on.

*** PART ONE ***

I was walking by the local kinky fetish gear shop the other day and on a whim I vent in. I don't usually have any use for all that silly leather and vinyl gear, but the trap-on dildos are fun to look at, and there's always a few glossy magazines. I went ver to the magazine rack and saw the usual assortment of boring mags such as Secret", "Marquis" and "Skin Two". But then a new title caught my eye. There was nly one copy left and I quickly stooped down to scoop it up: "Castratrix Quarterly"! couldn't believe my eyes. I thought it must be some kind of a satire or prank, so I ook a closer look. As it began to dawn on me that this was the real thing I couldn't elp but pop a raging boner in my pants, which was embarrassing to say the least. I uickly went over to the check out counter in order to buy it and the cute young girl n tons of eye make-up, multi-colored hair, and multiple facial piercings, of course) ehind the counter noticed my highly aroused condition. She looked at the nagazine and then at me and said "you like this stuff, huh?" I gulped an awkward es, and she smiled and gave me a wink and told me to enjoy myself.

I scooted out of the store and then back to my apartment at top speed. Once nside my apartment I quickly tore off my shoes and pants and sat down to read the nagazine, one hand holding the magazine while the other started stroking between ny legs.

The cover showed a proud and haughty looking dominatrix standing with her ands on her hips next to a kneeling naked man wearing only a leather bondage nask. His crotch was shaved and as he knelt his legs were spread and he held his ubbery looking cock up so that one could get a good look beneath it to see the mpty spot where his balls used to be. The caption read: "Helping Him Make His acrifice".

The first page had a couple introductory remarks by the editrix, Veronika van elder, about what an exciting time it was to be alive what with all our new sexual eedoms, and now, finally, castratrixes and their eunuchs could finally come out of ne their closets, too. And she ended her remarks by saying that her husband, Dave, ends his regards to all her readers. "It's been 5 years since I had my dear, sweet ave castrated, and we both couldn't be happier!"

The first article was called, "Live-in Eunuchs". This was a story about a dominant woman who lived in a nondescript house in suburbia with her 3 eunuch slaves. They did all the household chores, gardening and yard work, and also serviced her orally whenever she needed it. They all had jobs, as well, and their salaries were all given to their mistress. A few photos accompany the story showing this unusual menage contentedly at work and at rest in their shared house. One photo shows the mistres cheekily lifting up one of her eunuch's apron while he is cooking to take a quick pee at his shaved and ball-less crotch.

The second article was called, "Trophy Huntress". This was about a woman who gets off on seducing submissive men and then manipulating them into getting castrated for her. Once she has her trophy jar with their balls floating in it she ditches them and moves on to her next conquest. The photo that runs with the article shows the huntress' face half in shadow, with her trophy case, with row afte row of balls in specimen jars, in the background.

The third article was called, "Stable Boys". This was about a very athletic and confident young lady who ran her own horse ranch where she specialized in raising stallions. Occasionally one of her stallions would prove to be too unmanageable an she would have to call her friend, a lady vet, to come and have him gelded. Since al the hired hands on the ranch were males, she also discovered that this was an idea way of dealing with unruly men as well. She remembered the first time this happened. She was having a heated dispute with one of her hired hands, and she said, "you know Jim, if you were one of my stallions, I'd call the vet and have her come over and take care of you." She was astounded to find that Jim was only too willing to comply. Now, half the hands that work on her ranch have been gelded. The photo that ran with the story shows a naked man bending over a wooden rail i the stable with the lady vet going to work between his legs while the lady ranch owner looks on with smug satisfaction.

The fourth article was the cover story and contained a lot of helpful and sound advice to prospective castratrixes on how to best help their slaves get psychologically prepared to go through with the necessary surgery.

In the center of the magazine was a multi-page pictorial spread showing a number of mistresses posing with their submissive eunuch slaves.

There were a couple castration themed cartoons, too. One was of a man who was about to be branded and gelded along with the other horses in a corral. Anoth was of a very worried looking man with his balls and scrotum locked securely into a scaled down guillotine, with a devilish looking dominatrix holding the blade-release cord.

There were classifieds in the back, of course. These were divided into two sections: "Castratrix seeking male" and "Male seeking castratrix". Of course the second section was much larger than the first.

A few news items were given about the burgeoning castratrix/eunuch lifestyle. ome municipalities had legalized elective castration, most notably, San Francisco. A ew castration clinic based in San Francisco was also given a short blurb and a photo all female staff, of course. A private castration party held in San Francisco was also riefly mentioned.

By the time I'd got done reading the mag I must have cum at least 7 times and I ad to go and lay down in a semi-stupor for a couple hours just to recover from the ntensity of it.

*** PART TWO ***

After discovering the mind-blowing turn-on of the, "Castratrix Quarterly", at the ocal kinky fetish boutique, I went back and checked for new issues very frequently. oo frequently, especially considering it only came out 4 times a year. Every time I vent in I noticed that they seemed to be adding more and more castration related nerchandise to their stock on display. First it was a burdizzo, then an elastrator, nen an assortment of neuticles, then specimen jars with bottles of preserving fluid, nd so on. It was very fascinating for me, but at the same time very disturbing.

Then I began to notice haughty, dominant looking women coming into the shop ccompanied by submissive, self-effacing men and being escorted to a door in the ack of the shop. Once, the shop girl caught me staring at one of these strange ouples as she led them, and she turned and gave me a wicked smile and a devilish vinkle in her eye. I looked away quickly and felt my cheeks burn hot with shame nd embarrassment.

Later, as I was getting ready to leave, the shop girl came over to me and asked ne if I was interested in the new items that they were selling. Then she said, "you now, we're having a special photo shoot next week and we're looking for models. he photographers from, "Castratrix Quarterly", are coming for a special shoot in elebration of the grand opening of a new facility we've installed downstairs. Do you nink you might be interested?"

I had quickly developed an uncontrollable erection as soon as she started talking, nd I blushed hotly and became very flustered, but I managed to stammer, "Yes, of ourse, yes, but I don't, I hope we don't, they don't, I don't want to get too involved, arried away, out of hand, you know..."

The shop girl just smiled sweetly and told me not to worry and that if I just elaxed then I would probably really enjoy myself.

"What kind of facility is it," I asked, although I already had a strong hunch what ne answer was.

"Oh, it's our new submissive male body mods salon," she said easily. "You

yourself must be fully aware of how popular this lifestyle choice has become, so yo see we're simply filling a need."

Next week I showed up at the appointed hour and was quickly ushered downstairs to the male body mods salon. In a trice I was stripped naked. I looked around and the room was full of proud haughty statuesque cheerful laughing women. No other men. I was quickly locked into bondage stocks. Then my genitals were shaved and handled very familiarly by a confident young woman in a white medical smock. I soon developed an uncontrollable erection which was completely exposed to the highly amused women. Continually roving around in the backgroun was a photographer constantly photographing everything.

One of the women, in a very mocking voice, observes that I seem to be very aroused and asks me if I'd liked to be milked of my sperm. I tell her that I would rather not because that would be extremely embarrassing for me in front of all these women.

"You mean that you would find it embarrassing to be made to shoot out all of your private male essence in front of all of us women?"

"Yes, yes, that's exactly what I mean," I say as I struggle to escape from the bondage stocks. The stocks hold me fast, and the women laugh and taunt me as they take turns slowly manually teasing me and stroking me until I can no longer hold back and am forced to surrender to my ejaculation in front of all those womer They clap and laugh and smile and spank me on the butt as they watch all of my male essence shoot out from my bursting purple cock. I had never felt so open, so naked and exposed in my life. After the last throbs of my orgasm subsided I sagged weakly in the stocks, totally drained and exhausted by the experience. That's when heard the clink of metal on metal as a small cart was wheeled up behind me.

"We hope you enjoyed that orgasm, little man," said one of the ladies, "because now we're going to ask you to give us one more little show for our photographic shoot."

Just then I felt the sting and pinch of a hypodermic needle being jabbed into my scrotum. I well knew what kind of show they were referring to and I begged and pleaded with them not to do it to me.

One of the ladies laughed and rubbed by bottom to calm me down and said, "There, there, just relax and let it happen. After all, it wouldn't be very fair to all of us here celebrating this grand opening, or to the photographers from, "Castratrix Quarterly", if we weren't able to actually put this facility to the use for which it was intended, now would it?"

I could feel someone start to cut into my scrotum and I began to panic even mo and to whine and whimper and beg some more for them to please not to do it to n

ıd to let me go and to find someone else to do it to.

"Just think," the same lady continued, "next month it will be you on the front ›ver of "Castrartix Quarterly"! We won't show your face, of course, but we will be ving a very prominent view of your cute little butt and your freshly sewn up little rotum!"

Just then I heard the woman who was working on me between my legs say, "Ok, at's one. One down and one to go."

I softly moaned, "noooooo, noooooo, please," while all the women watched and niled and chatted and laughed as the photographer clicked steadily away.

Next month, I quietly slipped into the boutique to check out the latest "Castratrix uarterly". The shop girl spotted me and came over and picked up a copy from the ck. She looked at the photo of the naked man locked in bondage stocks on the ›ver, she looked at his cute butt and freshly sewn-up scrotum. Then she smiled and inked at me and handed me the magazine and said, "Go on, this one's free, it's on e house. Go on and take it home and enjoy yourself."

On the way out I notice a new display behind the check out counter. It was a ecimen jar up on a shelf with a sign saying, "Our male body mods salon first ficial customer." I sighed as I looked at the two round pinkish white objects ›ating in the preserving liquid and then turned and shuffled away.

. MANHOOD POUCH

My name's Dorkus Malorkus, and this is my story.

One day, while reading the ultra-kinky fetish mag, Castratrix Quarterly, I noticed ad for something called The Clinic. The ad said, "Have you ever dreamed of rrendering your manhood to a cruel and efficient castratrix? Come explore your epest, most forbidden castration fantasies. All our procedures are quick, painless d over before you know it. But be warned, no male who has entered our eatment plan has left with his manhood intact! Fees are negotiated after mpletion of treatment." This sounded too good to be true so I called the number d made an appointment.

When I called to make the appointment the receptionist's tone was initially quite ld and almost belligerent. Then she came right out and asked me point blank if I d a castration fetish. This really threw me and left me sputtering for half a minute fore I was able to answer in the affirmative. After that her manner changed mpletely and she became very warm and friendly.

On my first visit the receptionist handed me a 30 page questionnaire and

ushered me into a small private room with a desk and a chair. The first couple page covered general background information but the bulk of it was about my sex life: m history, experiences, hang-ups, preferences and above all, fetishes. Four whole pages at the end of the questionnaire where dedicated to asking specific, detailed questions about my castration fetish.

After I finished filling out the questionnaire I gave it to the receptionist and she told me to take a seat in the waiting room and that the doctor would see me short

After a few minutes a sexy lady doctor comes out into the waiting room and ca my name. I follow her into her office.

Her office is fairly large and includes the doctor's desk and an examination table I notice my questionnaire is lying on the desk in front of the doctor. The doctor tell me the exam table is where her patients surrender their manhood to her. "It's amazing how many men are eager to offer their manhood to me," she says.

I can't help but notice the rows of small jars arrayed on well-lit glass shelves in a large display case at the back of the office. The doctor notices where I'm looking ar smiles. She tells me that that's her manhood collection. Each jar is full of liquid and floating in each are a pair of roundish white things. She invites me to go over and pick one up. I see that a man's name and a date are printed on a label on top of ea jar.

The doctor tells me there are 3 lady doctors in The Clinic, all accomplished castratrixes, and that all the staff are female.

I timidly contradict her and tell that I had noticed a janitor while I was seated in the waiting room who wasn't female.

"Oh, that would be Joe," she said with a sly smile, "it's true, he's not female, bu he's also not male." Just then the door to the office opened and the janitor came i to empty the waste basket. "Oh, here's Joe now, let's ask him. Joe?"

"Yes, ma'am," he answered quietly.

"We were just talking about you and I was telling Mr. Malorkus here that you're not really a male. That's right, isn't it?" asked the doctor.

"Yes, Ma'am," said the Joe, somewhat sulkily.

"And why aren't you a male?" asked the doctor brightly.

"Because I no longer have my manhood," answered Joe, looking down at the floor.

"Oh dear, Joe," said the doctor, looking at me with a sly twinkle, "what ever

appened to your manhood?"

"You... you took it, doctor! You opened up my, my... and, and... you took my nanhood!" said Joe, balling up his fists, squeezing his eyes shut and giving an nguished gasp.

"Oh yes, now I remember. And you had a nice big pair, as I recall. And where is our manhood now, Joe?" she asked.

Joe raised his right arm and mutely pointed over at the display case.

"Very good, Joe. You may go," said the doctor, somewhat impatiently.

"Thank you, ma'am," said Joe, then he meekly shuffled out of the room, closing he door behind him.

The doctor turns to me and says, "Ok, Mr. Malorkus, take off all your clothes and et up on the exam table. I want to examine your manhood pouch."

When I look uncertain the doctor intuits my confusion and says, "Here at The linic we call the scrotum your manhood pouch, or pouch, for short."

I do as she says and climb naked up onto the exam table, lying on my back and utting my feet up in the stirrups. She compliments me on my tight pouch and the ig pair inside. As she gently caresses my pouch, she leans forward, looks me In the ye and tells me, almost in a whisper, that she looks forward to opening my pouch nd taking my manhood. Then, somewhat abruptly, she declares that my pouch is oo hairy and must be shaven. She calls one of her assistants to come shave me.

As the assistant is shaving me she also compliments me on my pouch and its ontents. She asks the doctor if she's planning on opening my pouch today. The octor replies, "Not today. Mr. Malorkus isn't quite ready yet. But I'm confident he vill be soon."

After I'm shaven and the assistant leaves the room the doctor orders me to keep ny manhood pouch shaven so as to facilitate its being opened when the time omes. All these allusions to castration cause me to become very aroused. My cock rock hard and dripping. "Really, Mr. Malorkus!" she exclaims, mildly outraged at ny exhibition. Then she tells me she doesn't mind if want to relieve myself so I grab old and urgently jerk off while she watches. After I finish the doctor hands me a ox of wet wipes.

Since I wasn't ready yet I had to undergo castration preparedness training. For nis I was sent to The Farm, a special facility owned and operated by The Clinic. After vo months I was judged to be ready. I was returned to The Clinic where I climbed p onto the doctor's special table and anxiously offered up my manhood. After I ecovered I was given Joe's old position of eunuch janitor.

18. MEN TO BOYS

Slim and effeminate, Billy Jones sits at his desk in his dorm room studying calculus. It's early evening and the room is dark except for a small desk lamp.

He hears a light knock at the door. He says, "Come in," and his pudgy, plain, dark haired girlfriend, Donna, enters.

"Hello, Billy," says Donna, softly and sweetly, "have you been behaving yourself?

"Y...yes, mommy." (Donna has trained Billy to call her mommy)

"I'd better have a look," says Donna, bossily, sitting down on Billy's bed.

"Please, mommy, it's so embarrassing!" whines Billy.

"Stop whining, Billy, and come over here so I can open your pants," Donna orders.

Billy comes over to stand meekly in front of her. She casually opens his pants.

"Oh my goodness, Billy! Just look at you! Your private part is so red and swollen! It's sticking straight up! Can't you control yourself!?" says Donna, mock accusingly.

"I'm sorry, mommy, I can't help it!" cries Billy.

"Just imagine, exposing yourself like this, right in front of me!" scolds Donna, "you should be very ashamed of yourself." Donna knows Billy loves being manhandled like this.

"Oh, oh, I'm, I'm sorry, mommy," whines Billy. A small bead of precum forms on the tip of his cock.

"And your hairy little bag is so tight and wrinkly. Have you been keeping it nice and full for me?" asks Donna, archly.

"Oh, oh, yes, mommy!" gasps Billy, involuntarily jerking his hips and thrusting his cock towards her.

"And just look at your hands," says Donna, "fidgeting like that. I know what you want to do. I know what dirty little boys like to do with their hands."

"Oh! Mommy!" gasps Billy.

"You want to touch it, don't you?" says Donna, "You want to grab it and rub it, don't you?"

"Y...yes, mommy, yes, I do, I... I can't help it!" cries Billy.

"What a dirty little boy to want to do that in front of a girl," says Donna, mock ffended, "to expose yourself and play with yourself like that."

"But, but mommy, I... I need to so bad... and you, you make me do it!" pleads illy.

"You know what bad, dirty boys call it, don't you? They call it jerking off. Is that ou want to do, Billy, jerk off?" Donna asks, accusingly.

"Oh, oh, yes mommy, I'm sorry, but please, please let me, let me do it..." begs illy.

"Alright then," says Donna, matter-of-factly, "sit down in the chair and do it. But e sure and keep your legs spread nice and wide."

Billy does as he's told.

To tease and excite him Donna pretends to call Billy's mother to discuss his utrageous sexual conduct.

After she gets off the phone Donna tells Billy that his mother had the exact same roblem with his dad a few years ago. "She gave me the name of a female specialist ho can help," says Donna, impishly.

Then Donna leans forward and gently grasps Billy's scrotum and starts to hythmically squeeze. "Are you ready to give your mommy a nice big, creamy load?" ne purrs.

Billy shudders and starts helplessly spurting. Donna watches and smiles while ontinuing to caress and squeeze his tight, aching bag. "What a good little boy to ive your mommy such a nice big, creamy load," she says.

On another occasion, while Billy sits and jerks off for her, Donna pretends to call ne female specialist to discuss treatment options for his sex habits. She makes an ppointment for him in two weeks. Billy continues to jerk off and gives Donna nother big, creamy load.

Two weeks later Donna tells Billy it's time to go for his appointment with the emale specialist.

"But I... I thought... it was just pretend?" says Billy, puzzled and confused.

"Oh, don't be such a fussbudget, Billy," says Donna, "I've spoken to her and she's ery nice. She just wants to take a quick look at you and ask a few questions. And I now you'll like her, she's very sexy."

At the specialist's office, Billy and Donna stand in front of the reception desk. Th doctor's assistant, a cute young girl, sits behind it.

The young assistant asks them with a devilish grin, "Is this the boy that likes to jerk off?"

Billy hangs his head in shame and blushes furiously. Both girls laugh.

Donna reaches down and rubs his bottom, then slides her fingers down to nudg up between the cleft, firmly and repeatedly prodding him in his most sensitive rear spot, making him pant, quiver and squirm.

Donna whispers to the young assistant, "I think he's ready to do it right now!"

"Oooh, can I see!" squeals the young assistant.

"Go on, Billy," says Donna, "take it out and show it to the nice girl."

Billy blushes and shyly opens his pants and takes it out. It stands up straight and hard, the head a dark purple looking ready to burst. Donna pushes his pants and underpants down so that his tight, wrinkly sac is also fully exposed.

"Oooh, you've got a nice one!" the young assistant exclaims gleefully.

Billy fidgets, clenching and unclenching his fists at his sides.

"Poor Billy", Donna says mockingly, "you really want to grab it and rub it, don't you?"

Just then the sexy female specialist comes out of her office and interrupts. She scolds the young assistant and warns her to be more careful about allowing patient to make sloppy messes.

Once in the examination room the specialist instructs Billy to take off his lower clothes, sit down and start masturbating. She, Donna and the young assistant, all seated comfortably, sit and watch.

The specialist compliments him on what a fine, stiff erection he has and what a nice, fat pair of family jewels he has.

The specialist tells Billy she remembers meeting his father and that he had the same sex habits. "I explained the therapeutic options to your mother. Unfortunate your father found it hard to accept the option she chose. But together we helped him realize we loved and cared for him. And it's quite a simple, easy procedure."

"Your dad had a lovely pair of family jewels, too, nice and fat and round," says the specialist with a giggle. "Your dad was such a sweet, trusting little boy on that day, offering his soft little bag to me. He looked at me with such love and devotion

I used my scalpel to gently open him up and take the two little sex glands that ere his manhood. After I sewed him up I played with his floppy little empty bag for while before bandaging it. And of course your mom enjoyed watching, too."

Bending forward in her chair the specialist reaches out to lightly caress Billy's ght sac as he continues to urgently stroke himself. "And of course you realize, Billy, at soon it'll be time for me to open your little sac, too," she says, her voice low and isky.

When Billy hears this he moans and starts spurting wildly while the women atch and smile. When it's over the young assistant hands him some wet wipes.

"Oh Billy," says Donna, "I can't wait! I know you'll look so cute afterwards. Your tle empty bag will be all sad and droopy. And just think, she did your dad! Your om had your dad castrated!"

"And he thanked me afterwards", says the specialist smugly. "They always do. side every man is a little boy that secretly yearns to offer his soft little bag to ommy so she can open it and pluck his aching manhood, making him her good tle angel forever. Billy'll be a good little boy too, once he's nice and castrated. I ve transforming men into sweet little boys."

. MOM HAS ME CASTRATED

Five naked, big-bottomed, sissy eunuchs waddled out onto the stage at the inuch auction. Their nipples and their rubbery little penises were stained a bright d, thus accentuating their submissive status. The auction is well attended by pper-class woman curious about the latest trend in domestic help.

Lady Nuttingham, the presenter, came on stage and said, "Welcome ladies, to is month's eunuch auction! And what a fine selection of eunuchs we have for you day!" There were a few titters from the audience. She paused, then said, "You ow, eunuchs make excellent servants and their castrated state serves as a nstant reminder of their subservient role. And you couldn't ask for sweeter, more rdworking and obedient personal servants. They're all fully trained to do all your usework and to serve you and your guests." And then, in a confidential semi-hisper, "They've also been trained to provide more intimate bedroom service, as ell." There were some gasps and ooohs at this. Then she announced cheerily, "And think, just a short time ago they were all lazy masturbators!" A ripple of strained laughter ran through the audience.

Lady Nuttingham went up to the first eunuch and asked him to present himself. e stepped forward, spread his legs and lifted up his little penis to show off his npty scrotum. There was polite applause.

"What's your name, eunuch?" asked Lady Nuttingham.

"Sid," he replied.

"Well, Sid," continued Lady Nuttingham, "what were you doing a year ago?"

"I... I was sitting around my mom's house all day watching TV, looking at Internet porn and... and masturbating!" stammered Sid, and he blushed and tried to hide his face.

"What a bad, naughty boy you were!" exclaimed Lady Nuttingham in mock outrage. "And then what happened?"

"My mom got fed up and called the Sissy Care Camp ladies to come for me!" Sid gasped out. There were a few giggles in the audience.

"Oh my, that must have been quite a shock, wasn't it?" said Lady Nuttingham as Sid nodded meekly. "And how do you feel about it now?"

"Oh... oh... I'm... I'm very happy and grateful now," said Sid.

"Grateful for what, exactly," pressed Lady Nuttingham.

"For my mom having me castrated and trained by the ladies at the camp!" whimpered Sid.

"There, there, that's a good boy," soothed Lady Nuttingham. She then added slyly, "And I presume that you no longer have any masturbation problems, correct?" The audience laughed and the sissy eunuch hung his head in shame.

Then she told him to stand back in line. As he did so, he began to think back to that day when the he'd been picked up by the ladies from the Sissy Care Camp.

At the camp he was taken to an office where the director sat behind a desk with a sexy young nurse sitting beside it. There was a medical exam table with stirrups in the office. The director told him to be seated and introduced herself as Dr. Amelia Brown and her nurse as Maryann.

"Well, Sid," Dr. Brown began in a warm and friendly way, "I understand that you've been having certain behavioral problems."

"Yes, yes," stammered Sid.

"Well, don't worry, I'm confident we can help."

"Thank, thank you, doctor."

Becoming more serious she said, "It seems your main problem is your sexual ehavior. My notes here say you're a compulsive masturbator?" She looked at him nquiringly.

"I, I, no, I," babbled Sid, blushing furiously.

"But according to my notes it says you're in the habit of masturbating at least our times a day. That's correct, isn't it?"

"I, I... yes," Sid quietly said and hung his head in shame. The doctor smiled mugly.

"And when you masturbate, do you use pornography?"

"Yes."

"What kind."

"Sissy porn."

"And what kind of pornography is that?"

"That's, that's where strong women turn, turn men into weak sissies and umiliate them."

"I see. And it also says in my notes that you still live at home with your mother nd an older sister and that you are frequently 'caught in the act', so to speak. Not ust by them but by their female guests as well."

"I, I, yes, it's true, but, but mom is awful snoopy..." Sid spluttered.

"And it also says you expose yourself to your sister almost every day."

"Yes, but, but it's not fair!" exclaimed Sid in a near panic, "I can't help it! She nakes me do it!"

"You openly masturbate and ejaculate in front of her, is that true?"

"But, but, she, she teases me! And sometimes she even invites over her irlfriends and she makes me jerk off for them!" babbled Sid.

Dr. Brown cut him off, saying, "Now don't try and shift the blame onto others, id. After all, it was your sister's idea to send you to this camp."

Sid whimpered and slumped dejectedly.

Dr. Brown cleared her throat and said, "Well, it's just as I thought. First of all, I'm oing to enjoy nipping your little sexual problem right in the bud. Please get ndressed and lie down on my exam table."

"What, what are you going to do to me?" he asked anxiously as he did as he was told.

"I'll explain as we go along. Maryann, get his feet in the stirrups and shave his scrotum."

"You see, Sid, what boys like you fail to realize is that when you're caught doing dirty and naughty things you forfeit your manhood."

"Inject the anesthetic." Maryann injected both testicles.

"Since you can't use your male equipment properly I'm going to remove the problem."

"Oh no!" whimpered Sid, "please don't!"

"Relax, I have your mother's full approval. In fact, she specifically requested it. I've done it a lot, it won't take long."

The doctor went to work and in a few minutes it was over and Maryann bandaged him up.

"Welcome to Sissy Care Camp, Sid. You're now a eunuch," Dr. Brown said smugl Sid whimpered and the nurse giggled.

20. MY WIFE TAKES ME TO AUNT ABIGAIL'S

My wife hadn't given me sex in over a month. She began to get in the habit of teasing and exciting me whenever I got out of the shower. She would talk sexy to m and give me little peeks of her tits, ass and pussy. When I got hard she would giggle and say it looked like I really needed to get some relief. Then she would coyly ask m if I wanted to do it myself, by hand. I knew that the punishment for jerking off in ou town was to be taken to Aunt Abigail's to be 'trimmed' so I always resisted. But one day I was so hard and dribbling that I gave in and grabbed it and jerked it while my wife watched with excited delight. After I have an intense, shuddering ejaculation she tells me to clean myself up and get dressed because we are going for a ride. I as her where to and she says she'll tell me when we get there.

I am apprehensive when she parks the car in front of Aunt Abigail's. She tells me not to worry, that she was talking to Aunt Abigail about me and Aunt Abigail said she'd really like to meet me.

Once we get inside my wife introduced me to Aunt Abigail who says she has heard a lot about me and is really pleased to meet me. Then Aunt Abigail asks me i I'd like to see her trimmin' parlor in the back. Once there, she shows me her specia

·immin' chair. "When men do naughty things with their private parts they need to e trimmed. It's surprising how many of them do it. The most common thing is erking off."

She showed me her trimmin' shears. "And here's the little stainless steel bowl I ut your balls in."

Then she says my wife told her I have very nice private parts and she would really ke to see them. She tells me to take off my pants and underpants and sit in the hair. She tells me to spread my legs nice and wide. She tells me she has to strap my egs down so that they'll stay wide apart and make it easy for her to see my private arts. She compliments me on my private parts. To take a closer look at my nanhood pouch she tapes my cock up to my abdomen. She says she much prefers o see a cleanly shaved manhood pouch so she applies some shaving cream and haves mine. Then she takes a big hypodermic needle and injects my scrotum. I ask er why and she says it's so it won't hurt when she opens my manhood pouch.

"But why are you going to open my manhood pouch?" I ask.

"Because I want to take your manhood, Billy," she says with a smile.

"Please don't," I plead. "Is it because I jerked off this morning?"

"Oh, no," Aunt Abigail replied. "Many women in this town make their men jerk ff for their amusement and gratification."

"Then... then, why?" I asked.

"Well, because sometimes when I see a nice pair of balls I just want to take them, nd you have a very nice pair. And because your wife wanted me to."

I turned to my wife who had been watching and listening and asked, "Why?"

"You ask too many questions, but I'll it answer anyway. Because it would make ou easier to manage and because I wanted to see you turned into a meek little unuch."

"Just lay back and relax," said Aunt Abigail. "This won't take long."

1. ONLY SISSIES MASTURBATE

Before I met my wife I was thin and fit and I considered myself a normal, virile an. Now, thanks to the devious and wicked plans of my sly wife, I'm pudgy, with a g soft bottom and I crave being sexually used and humiliated by women and men. I specially crave being penetrated anally. And now she says she's thinking of having e castrated!

Right after we were married my wife told me that access to her 'gates of heave would be a rare privilege, and that only sissies masturbate.

I tried really, really hard to control myself but then one day it happened: she caught me red-handed, naked from the waist down and looking at Internet porn. She smiled and said, "Well, just look at the sissy enjoying himself!" Then, with a devilish grin she said, "I'm actually glad you like that because I'm going to make you do it like that from now on." Then she told me to do it while she watched. It was so humiliating and embarrassing to have to perform my most private sex function like that. When I finished she praised me and told me I was a good little sissy.

After that she put me on a special fattening diet and no-exercise regime that made my bottom really swell and grow.

Then one day I came out of the shower wearing a towel and she told me to com over to where she sat on the bed. She told me to turn around and take off the towe "Ummmm," she purred as she ran her hands over my bottom, "I just love how big and soft it is." I felt a strange mixture of excitement and fear.

Then she made me turn around and show my helpless hardness. She tutted and said what a naughty sissy I was. Then, with a devilish grin she said, "Go on, honey, take care of yourself... the way you like."

"Please, honey, don't..." I begged.

"Go on, be a good little sissy for mommy," she said. I burned with shame and humiliation as I took myself in hand. After I finished she rubbed and patted my bottom and praised me.

After that, she never lost an opportunity of teasing me about my bottom and drawing attention to it. At home she made me go around the house with it totally bare. She liked it to always be completely exposed and accessible to her wicked, knowing hands.

She spent a lot of time gently touching, squeezing and caressing my big soft bottom and training me to be sensitive and receptive. When she played with my bottom I could never resist the impulse to lean forward and stick it out, inviting her to take control. This involuntary reaction always made her laugh while I blushed an squirmed.

One day she slowly and gently ran her index finger up the cleft between my bottom cheeks and said, "Hmmmm, what's in here? I bet you've got something special hidden in here." I trembled and clenched my bottom and felt my nipples harden.

"Please, honey, don't..." I gasped.

"Ummmmmm, I can see I'm going to have fun with you," she purred.

She began to explore the tender cleft between my bottom cheeks. I trembled in nticipation. She spread my cheeks with one hand and began to gently rub and prod y quivering hole with the other. I begged her to stop but she just laughed softly. I alized she was gradually stripping me of my manhood but I was helpless to resist.

****

Whenever she had female friends over to visit she made me wait on them. Once, hile I was getting some things ready in the kitchen I overheard her talking to her iends.

"What do you think of hubby? Isn't he coming along nicely?" said my wife.

"Oh yes, what a nice big bottom!" said one of her friends and they all laughed.

My wife said, "Thanks. It was pretty easy, really. The first step was to train him to ke care of his own sex. I knew when I met him that he was the type who asturbates a lot. So when I caught him jerking off it was easy to shame him into oing it all the time." They all laughed.

"You're right, it's so easy to do that!" piped up one of her friends. "I trained all y boyfriends to do that. Men are such little boys, they love showing off for ommy!" They all laughed.

"Oh, I know," said another woman. "I love making a guy perform, especially when 's saved up a big load. It's so much fun watching him milk it out! It makes him so nbarrassed!" They all laughed.

I came into the room carrying a tray of drinks and snacks.

"Oh, hi dear," my wife said, "I was just discussing how much I enjoy making you rk off!" I blushed and stammered and they all laughed. Then she turned to one of r friends and said, "Oh, and Bernice, thanks for lending me a copy of Sissy Care, it ve me such wonderful ideas for transforming hubby, I'm going to subscribe."

"Oh, no problem," said Bernice, "I've used it on my hubby, too, of course. Some the ideas are a little extreme. Like having sex with another man while hubby atches. Or making hubby service another man. It is kinda exciting but, gee, I don't ow."

"Oh yeah, and how about the idea of 'fixing' his little masturbation problem," ickered my wife mimicking scissor snips with her index and middle finger, "like a ughty little doggy." The women gasped with shock and then started tittering.

"Don't laugh," said Bernice, "I know a woman who had her hubby 'fixed' and

she's quite happy with the result." There was a mixed reaction of shock, amuseme and curiosity.

Meanwhile, all this kind of talk had made me very excited, and my tight shorts bulged out in front as I stood at the side of the room. My wife noticed and whispered to some of the other ladies.

"Honey," my wife called out, "would you come here a minute?" I timidly walkec over. "Honey, I hope you don't mind, but I want to share you with my friends. Be a good little boy and take your sweet little sissy clitty out, OK?" I hesitated for a moment to make sure she was serious and then I reached down and started to unzip. My cheeks burned as I pulled it out to full exposure. All the women had beer holding their breath to see if I would do it. They all sighed and giggled after I'd don it.

"Oh, look at you," cooed my wife, "you're so stiff and hard! But let's get your balls out too." She reached into my shorts and gently pulled them out. Then she wiped off some of the wetness smeared around the tip and cooed, "Ooooooh, loc how excited you are! You're dripping!" Then she said, "OK now, honey, I want you clasp your hands behind your back and go stand in front of each of my friends and present yourself so they can get a real good look. But no 'accidents', OK?"

The first woman I presented myself to smiled and said, "My, what a sweet and obedient hubby you are!" Then she looked up at me with a devilish grin and reache out and gently squeezed my balls. "Ummmm, your balls are so tight and full!" The women laughed. She gently curled the soft fingers of her other hand around my throbbing stiffness. I almost swooned with pleasure. She watched my face carefull as she gave it a gentle squeeze and a couple slow strokes.

After enduring a couple more handlings like this I couldn't stand it anymore anc begged my wife to let me go and relieve my urgent need. She told me she was disappointed but she finally relented. I felt so ridiculous, running out of the room with my stiff, dripping cock wobbling in front of me. They all laughed. "Come back when you've finished!" called my wife.

After recovering from a very intense ejaculation I went back in. As I got near I could hear quiet talk and occasional laughter. As I timidly entered they became qu and expectant. With a sly, knowing smirk my wife asked me if I felt better now. I ju hung my head and they burst out laughing merrily.

Then my wife turned to one of her friends and said, "Audrey, what were you saying about the woman who had her husband castrated?"

"Oh yes," said Audrey, "she's my neighbor. I was visiting and somehow the subject came up. When she saw how interested I was she had her husband lower h pants so I could see what he looked like. His peepee was small and childish and

here was nothing underneath except two small scars."

"Wow!" said my wife, "you're so lucky! I've never even known a man who's been astrated."

"Oh, they're more common than you think," said Bernice. "Many women are hoosing it. I've even discussed it with my Arnold."

2. PA LOSES HIS NUTS

"C'mon, Pa", says Ma. "Let's go out to the barn. I'm gonna take them nuts off ya."

"Aw, c'mon, Ma", says Pa, "you can't be serious".

"Now, you know what I told you, Pa, if I caught you exposin' yerself to Little Sis gain."

"I'm sorry, Ma, you know me, I couldn't help myself, it just felt so darn good!"

"This is the last time, Pa. Now let's go."

Out in the barn Ma tells Pa to pull off his pants and underpants and then tells him o sit in a wooden chair and spread his legs. She puts a rubber band tight and high p around Pa's nut sack to control the bleeding. Then she fits a wooden box with a pring-loaded slicing blade inside around his nut sack. It pinches a little going on and a says, "Ouch!"

Ma tells Pa he might as well have one last cum before she cuts his nuts off, so she ells him to jerk off.

Ma stands with her hands on her hips watching Pa jerk off and shoot a big load hat splatters on the barn floor. Then she bends over and pushes a button on the ide of the box. Pa hollers in pain as his whole nut sack is sliced neatly off. She wraps e stub of his nutsack with a bandage.

Ma says, "I'm sorry I had to do that to ya, Pa, but I had no choice".

"I understand", says Pa, as he gingerly pulls on his pants.

Ma pulls Pa's severed nutsack out of the slicing box and says, "I'm gonna tan this. our nutsack is gonna make a nice change purse".

"Whatcha gonna do with my nuts, Ma?" says Pa.

"Oh, feed 'em to the hogs, I guess."

"How many men have you de-balled with that contraption?" says Pa.

"Fifteen, countin' you", says Ma.

"Who's next?" asks Pa.

"Bubba Johnny, probably", says Ma. "Little Sis told me the other day she caught him playin' with himself out behind the barn."

"Do you remember buildin' this nut-slicing box for me five years ago?" says Ma.

"Yep", says Pa, "I do".

23. PREPPING A PIGGY-BOY

Summary: A peephole view into a day in the life of a joyous and unabashed Castratrix.

I stand a few feet away from the naked piggy-boy lying on his back on my specia medical play table. I note with approval how his legs are kept bent back, high up an wide apart by the stirrups. I let my eyes linger on his freshly shaved genitals and puckered butt hole that are now so totally vulnerable and exposed to me. I stand nearly naked myself. I wear only comfortable flat sandals, a black bra and a strap-o dildo. I lube the dildo up and then move in toward my target, his tight and tender butt hole.

He knows what's coming and moans softly as the head of my plastic cock finds it's target between his soft parted butt cheeks. I think to myself of all the piggy-boy that I have done this too, all the piggy-boys that have been sent to me for this special treatment by their wives, or girlfriends, or mistresses, or dominatrixes -- the owners, in other words. They know I am the best and that I always deliver on that very special treatment they require for their little piggy-boy pets.

I ease the dildo slowly into him and watch with satisfaction as his cock grows fatter and harder. I lube his cock and start gently stroking it in my right hand, matching the rhythm with that of my hips as I begin to fuck his ass with the strap-o I like to start out slow and then build to a shattering climax. I've found that that's th best way to make a tense little piggy-boy become really nice and loosened up, opened up and receptive to what I am secretly planning to do to him next.

Sure enough, a half an hour later, my tender victim is almost half mad with the pleasure I am giving him in his ass and cock. He moans and shudders and begs me t fuck him harder, just like a slutty little whore. I grin from ear to ear as I watch him surrender his sperm to me and spill it out over and over in thick hot spurts onto his chest and belly.

After the tremors of his climax have subsided, he lapses into a half stupor and I ently ease the dildo out of him. His legs are relaxed and spread, his asshole lose and hrobbing, and his cock and balls completely drained and limp. I well know that a iggy-boy is totally receptive and trusting at this moment. He thinks that the session all over now, now that he is well satisfied.

That is when I reach under the table and pull out a hypodermic syringe and inject is groin area with a powerful local anesthetic. He is so out of it that he barely otices it. My sexy little assistant, Wendy, then steps forward with the tray holding ny stainless steel surgical instruments and I quickly and deftly begin my work. A few ninutes later, as I sew up the little piggy-boy's newly empty scrotum, I smile to nyself, thinking how deliciously ironic it is that so many little piggy-boys sub-onsciously associate being well dildo fucked with having undergone a virtual astration.

I then tell Wendy to wheel the cute little ball-less piggy-boy out so that he can be icked up by his very dominant female owner. Still in a half stupor, he groggily runts out an inquiring noise. The silly little piggy-boy doesn't even realize yet what's een done to him! That realization will come a little later, when his owner gets him ome and the anesthetic begins to wear off. I've been told that the frantic panic and esperate pleading that the little piggy-boy pet makes when he does realize what's een done to him is highly amusing, and erotically stimulating, to their owners. One f my clients even video taped her freshly castrated piggy-boy with a hidden video amera and then sent me a copy. I have to admit that I found the silly little piggy-oy's desperate anguish and distress to be highly amusing and sweetly erotic, too. I till slip the video tape into my VCR every now and then and watch it when I want to njoy a quiet moment of solo pleasure alone with my vibrator. In fact, I'm getting et just thinking about it right now. Hmmmm, nice, very nice.

All the piggy-boys that I do are required to come back to see me again in a nonth's time for a follow-up check-up. Wendy and the dominant female owner and always enjoy these appointments. The piggy-boy always looks so hurt and resentful s we make him drop his pants and spread his legs and hold his penis up out of the ay so that we can all take a good long look at the flat empty space where his balls sed to be. Not content just to look, I always make a point of, somewhat roughly, ouching and feeling all around his scrotal area.

Sometimes the little piggy-boy will even whimper out a peevish and petulant ttle accusation while we are inspecting him. Something like: "You shouldn't have one it to me, ya know. Why'd ya have to do it, why'd ya take my balls like that?" sually his dominant female owner will respond in a gentle, but firm, voice: "Now illy, we've been through this already. You knew when you signed the agreement to e my full-time pet that having you fixed was, according to the fine print, one of the ptions that I was free to exercise. And I also warned you on at least two separate ccasions about your bad habit of openly touching yourself in front of me and my

other dominant female friends. I distinctly remember warning you that bad little piggy-boys who openly play with their naughty private pee-pees shouldn't be surprised when they get taken to the vet. Besides, you well know yourself that bein neutered has made you a much better pussy-licker. You should be content that you now enjoy the privilege of eating out my pussy and all my girlfriends' pussies and stop complaining just because I had you castrated and you can't get a hard-on anymore."

Snapping out of my daydream, I look up to see that Wendy has ushered in a nev freshly shaven little piggy-boy and is busy getting him ready and up onto my specia table. When he is relaxed and in the required position, Wendy half turns to me and gives me a little wink and a sly smile, which I quietly return. Wendy enjoys watching me at work almost as much as I enjoy carrying it out. She's a very bright and eager girl, and I've promised to teach her how to do sneaky quickie castrations on piggy-boys so that she too can open a special clinic of her own some day. She just loves watching me open up a plump, ripe looking scrotum and pop out the testicles and then snip them off, and, of course, I just love doing it, too.

We have 10 more piggy-boys yet to do today, so I put a new condom on my dildo, lube it up and then move on in to penetrate the naive and trusting little piggy boy's eager, welcoming, tight little butt hole. As I start to slowly thrust my hips back and forth, fucking him, I can't suppress a giggle when he breathlessly thanks me for what I am doing to him.

24. PROPERTY TRANSFER

Summary: It's that time special time again when Victoria gets to choose her nex neutered oral sex slave. Of course the selection process itself is half the fun.

Victoria entered the room with three of her favorite girlfriends. She walked casually behind the row of naked males who were each tightly gagged and shacklec and bent over a long bench. She stopped behind each one to deftly reach between their legs and gently stroke and squeeze their smooth hairless scrotums. "Hmmm", she purred, "they're all so nice and big and fat and juicey, I don't know where to begin. It's such a shame that I'm only allowed to pick one to have done. I know this sounds greedy, girls, but I'd love to have about five done. That would just be so naughty and delicious!" Her friends giggled and snickered.

Finally she stopped behind one male with a particularly large bulging sac. She softly caressed it and gave it a couple light squeezes. "Ummmm," she purred, "this one's got a nice big set, I'll bet he's very proud of them." She turned and winked at her companions, "It'd be a real shame if he were to lose them, somehow, don't you

ink?"

They heard a desperate, muffled protest through the gag in the male's mouth ıd Victoria and her friends laughed merrily. "Uh oh," said Victoria wryly, "sounds :e this one's really pretty anxious to retain ownership of his family jewels!" More tle fits of giggling erupt from the girls. "Well in a delicate case like this, I think that would probably be for the best if some very special measures were taken in order ensure and preserve their safekeeping. They look to me to be pretty exposed and ılnerable as they are now. What do you think, girls, don't you think that this young an's most prized possessions would be a lot safer if we were able to find a more ecure place to keep them? A place where they'd be safe from certain wicked and eaky ladies who might try and take them away?"

Victoria reached into her pocket and took out an elastic band with a large tag anging from it and with a delighted little laugh she deftly slipped the band around e male's soft wrinkly sac and let it snap tightly around it.

More desperate, pleading sounds came from behind the male's gag as he ruggled helplessly against his bonds.

Victoria laughed merrily at the male's impotent struggles and dropped one hand nto the right side of his rump and softly and soothingly caressed it. "Awww, poor ing, I think he knows what he's being selected for, she said to her friends. "Now on't worry sweetheart," she purred to the male, "all my lady friends on the medical aff here are very gentle and highly skilled and it'll all be over before you know it ıd you won't feel a thing." Her hand moved around to curl around his warm pink rotum again. She let it linger there, enjoying the feel of it in her hand and relishing er power over this big powerful man. She squeezed gently and felt the balls slide ound inside their sac. "Hmmmm", she purred, "you do have a very nice set. And on't you worry about my keeping them safe. I've got a special locked metal cabinet here I keep all the pairs of family jewels that are entrusted to me."

She turned to her friends and said, "After he's been given a few weeks to cover, I'll have him brought to my bedroom. I look forward to feeling his obedient ngue licking my hot slippery slit. Nothing compares to the thrill of having a brand w eunuch use his servile and obedient tongue to pay oral tribute to one."

Then, turning away she said, "Now how about lunch?" She and her friends began chat as they walked away.

The tagged male continued to struggle desperately and to make muffled pleas rough his gag.

All of a sudden, Victoria stopped and said, "Wait a minute girls, I almost forgot." ıd she pulled out her cell phone and punched in a number. Standing several yards vay from the row of naked men, she began to speak on the phone. "Yes," she said

as her eyes came to rest on the big tag dangling from the protruding scrotum of th male she had selected, "I just got done choosing the one I want. He's all ready for you to pick up. What? Do I what? Why yes, I would like to watch this one getting snipped. Yes, as usual. So let me know when you're ready to do him and I'll be righ over, OK? Thanks again, bye!"

And then she turned back to rejoin her friends and they slowly walked, chatting as they went, toward to exit and thence on to the restaurant they had chosen for lunch. She felt in the mood for Thai today, for some reason.

25. RETIRING AN OLD SPERM BULL

He was led naked into the special stall by the uniformed female handlers. The lady vet was already there, waiting.

He had served them well and had surrendered countless thick, heavy loads to their firm, milking hands.

He didn't struggle as they bent him over to lock his head in the stanchion. His genitals had grown abnormally large from continuous use. They made him spread his legs so his genitals were accessible from behind.

One of the handlers stepped forward to milk him. She took her time and made last. Finally, with a strangled grunt, two drops of seed dribbled out. His production had fallen way off.

The lead handler apologized for what they were about to do, but it was felt it w best that he should be permanently relieved of his sperm producing duties.

The lady vet moved to stand behind him. She reached between his legs and injected his big, hanging balls with anesthetic. The handlers stood around and watched as she gently cut open his scrotum and then slowly and lovingly gelded hi

Then they released the new steer from the stanchion and led him out to the special enclosure reserved for gelded bulls.

That night, the vet stayed for dinner at the sperm farm. The vet and the handle sat around the dining room table and laughed and joked about the new steer as th enjoyed a special stir fry that featured tender, sliced testicles. The vet had a hearty appetite and she asked for a second helping.

26. SATURDAY AFTERNOON

I'd just taken a shower and was mostly dried off but I was still walking around

aked.

My girlfriend was sitting fully-clothed in the living room. She watched me walking round and started to talk.

GF: "I wonder what you would look like if you were castrated."

I was a bit shocked but I knew she'd recently discovered my secret castration etish.

GF: "I think your little peeny will look so cute sticking out all by itself with no alls. And oh, look! Your little peeny is getting stiff so I can see you're interested. Why don't you sit and play with yourself while we talk."

I sat down and spread my legs for her. I took my stiffening cock between my humb and fingertips.

GF: "You've thought about it too, haven't you?"

I looked down and blushed.

GF: She smiled. "Don't be embarrassed. Lots of women have eunuchs. Two of my est friends have them. And I've seen them naked. My friends made them pull their ants down and spread their legs so I could get a good look at their little empty sacs nd cute, rubbery peenies. I could tell it was very humiliating for them but we just aughed."

GF: "I'd love to see you like that, with an empty sac and a cute peeny."

She smiled and I gasped.

GF: "Admit it, you want to be eunuch, don't you?"

All I could say was, "oh! oh!", as I I began to stroke myself more quickly.

GF: Watching my stroking hand she said, "You know, you won't be able to do that nymore after."

"What?" I asked.

GF: "Play with yourself. You won't be able to do that after I have you fixed," she aid with a devilish twinkle.

I started breathing heavily and wrapped my hand around my cock to stroke arder.

GF: "Just look at you, you're really into it. And of course you realize that by jaculating you'll be giving me consent."

"Oh no!" I gasped, stroking rapidly.

GF: "Uh hum," she purred.

"Oh no, please don't!" I begged. But it was too late, I yanked hard on my cock and started squirting all over.

GF: She smiled smugly and said, "Good. I knew you'd give your consent."

I shuddered with pleasure as I pumped out a few more dribbles.

Her smile gave me a chill. Her girlfriends really did have eunuchs.

27. SCROTUM POACHING

My name is Gloria Gelder and I'm a scrotum poacher.

I've always been interested in castration, partly because of my surname and partly because the idea fascinated and excited me.

I first learned about scrotum poaching when I was in high school. I volunteered t do an extra-credit project for biology class. My teacher, Mr. Hurlburt, expressed strong concerns when I told him what I wanted to study, which was primitive and unusual methods of castration, but I stubbornly refused to change it. Perhaps Mr. Hurlburt had a presentiment about my project. Poor Mr. Hurlburt.

A couple weeks later I was in the sub-basement of a nearby university library browsing their special collections archive. I was skimming over a translation of an ancient papyrus when I suddenly realized I'd stumbled onto something quite amazing. I had found the detailed, step-by-step instructions on how to perform the arcane and occult art of scrotum poaching. I was all a-tremble as I excitedly made copies of the text. I also couldn't wait to try it out for real.

When I finished my project I asked Mr. Hurlburt to allow me to present the results to him in an after-school meeting. We met in the biology classroom at the agreed time. The rest of the school was quite empty. When I described my findings about scrotum poaching he became visibly agitated. I smiled, patted him on the bottom and told him that perhaps a little demonstration was in order.

Poor balding, paunchy, bespectacled, middle-aged, unmarried Mr. Hurlburt. I told him to take off his pants and underpants and sit down on the edge of a chair with his legs spread. He hesitated at first and I was afraid he might try to resist but kept my cool and waited patiently. I smiled when he finally caved in and did it. I knelt down in front of him and began to firmly knead and pull on his proud and plump scrotum. His penis soon became erect. I told him to take hold of it and strok

And boy was mom pissed when she found out! So I just went out, bought her an extra-large vibrating dildo (with batteries) and told her to get over it. She really blew up and acted like she was going to murder me but I just kept my cool and told her it served him right, exposing himself like that to his own daughter. She never did forgive me and I ended up having to move out and go live with my aunt and uncle.

I poached a few of the adults in my town, but mostly it was boys my own age. It was then that I realized the puppy-like devotion a boy feels for the girl who poaches his scrotum. Every time I passed one of these boys in the hallway at school they'd give at me that sad, wistful look.

One day I asked one of my schoolboy eunuchs to follow me into the woods. When we reached a small clearing I pulled off my panties, sat down and leaned back against a tree. I spread my legs and lifted the front of my skirt, exposing my furry, glistening pussy. I told him to get down and lick me. It was then I discovered the exquisite pleasure of having my pussy licked by a gentle and obedient eunuch.

I'm thirty now and I work on a kinky porn magazine called "Castratrix Quarterly". Just the other day I came home from work feeling irritated and restless. I soon realized the ideal remedy for my bad mood. After a light supper I packed three scrotum storage receptacles into a small bag, got in my car and drove over to the next town.

A few hours later I was driving home, leaning back in my seat, relaxed, refreshed and satisfied, with all three receptacles filled. It'd been so easy. I had merely gone to a porn shop, a porn theater and a pick-up bar. Finding flabby, pimply losers who couldn't believe their luck was child's play. I took each one to a cheap motel where did the deed. They cried afterwards, but really, what could they do? Silly boys, thinking that a sexy, classy babe like me would take an interest in them. Those pathetic dweebs were way outta their league. They should've stuck to watching porno videos at home and pulling their pud. Anyway, when I got home I added their scrotums to my already impressive collection.

I've shown my scrotum collection to a few of my lady friends and they're very envious. Most of them also work at "Castratrix Quarterly". And I don't just work there, I'm the publisher and editrix-in-chief. They all begged me to teach them the dark art of scrotum poaching but I just smile. So, whenever my lady friends need to geld a guy they're stuck using cruder methods like surgery or the scrotum-guillotine Of course we've featured scrotum poaching a few times in "Castratrix Quarterly" but we've only hinted at how it's done. I don't think the world's quite ready for more than one scrotum poacher.

I hope you enjoyed my story and I also hope someday I'll get to meet you and add your scrotum to my collection.

Good-bye and take care,

3. SEDUCTION

The all-female Behavioral Quality team delivered the man, bound and struggling, the clinic. He was a big bull-of-a-man but the all-female clinic staff soon had him aked, gagged and trussed-up on the operating table.

His legs were bent double, they were raised up and spread wide. His arms were curely strapped down. His genitals were raised up, fully exposed and vulnerable.

The surgeon and her assistants were all good-looking women.

The surgeon began to speak:

It's a pity your kind of man isn't valued anymore, Mr. Jones. Your kind of dignity a liability. So proud and stubborn. Society is selectively breeding more pliable and reeable men all the time but there are still a few holdovers.

I've read your case file and it's clear you've been tolerated as long as possible. ow some serious adjustments are called for.

The root of your problem is well-known, it's the source of your strength and ale pride. Once it's removed you will be a lot easier to handle. You're a big, strong, ll-of-a-man now but soon you'll be a sweet, meek little steer.

* * * * *

A couple days later, the lady clinic director leads a small group of women rough the dayroom. A big man is sitting quietly at one of the tables. Indicating the an at the table she begins to speak:

Here is our latest castrate, Mr. Jones. How are we doing today, Mr. Jones? Still a tle sore?

Mr. Jones nods. The director continues:

He was brought in by the Behavioral Quality. Mr. Jones was quite a pigheaded, oublesome man but now there will be a complete change. It's very gratifying.

And in general, the ones I enjoy seeing the most are the ones that resist. They're raid to lose their manhood! It's quite amusing to us ladies. Soon, their little sac th be empty.

The ladies titter and the director continues:

I love running into our many castrates around town. They're always very friendly

and respectful.

Whenever I meet a man I always wonder what he'll be like castrated. Of course always make a point of telling him about my clinic. I smile and explain the benefits. tell him he might enjoy a consultation, many men do. I love when they take me up on my offer. It becomes a game of seduction.

More tittering. The director continues:

Here's what happens. I begin by asking if the idea turns him on. Then I instruct him to take his penis out and play with it while we talk.

The ladies gasp in surprise. The director continues:

He's embarrassed, of course, but I help him overcome it. I probe him about his interest until he admits his secret fascination. His hand begins to work more quickl on his penis. I tell him I've helped many men and I'd love to help him too. I quietly watch him ejaculate. Then I lead him into the operating room where the lady surgeon is waiting.

Well, I think that concludes our tour, ladies. And good-bye, Mr. Jones, I look forward to seeing you around town.

29. SEXUAL BEHAVIOR CONSULTANT

Summary: Stan has a problem maintaining his sexual composure during a medi exam. Luckily, the clinic recently acquired a new therapist to handle this.

I sat and fidgeted nervously in the clinic waiting room. I was waiting for my appointment with Dr. Sally Brown, the clinic's staff sexual behavior consultant. I ha never been to see a doctor like Dr. Brown before and had no idea what to expect.

I thought back to a week before when I had gone in to have my yearly physical. The nurse practitioner, Jane, had been examining my testicles for lumps when I found myself becoming hotly erect. The nurse practitioner straightened up, took a step back and looked at me as I stood there, my underpants down around my kne and my penis standing straight up, throbbing and obscenely on display. She excuse herself and left. She came back after a couple minutes and said that she had made an appointment for me with Dr. Brown, the staff sexual behavior consultant and asked if I would have any problems with keeping the appointment. I just gulped timidly and said, "No m'am, I'll go, if you think I should."

"Yes, Mr. Jones, I think that it would be for the best if you did," she responded.

he then gave me a sheet of paper with some printed instructions on what to do in reparation for my appointment.

The preparations for the appointment required me to eat only liquids the day efore and to give myself a Fleet enema in the morning, an hour before coming to he appointment.

I had done as instructed and now sat there in the waiting room feeling a little veak and empty. I looked around and noticed there were only a few other people itting in the waiting room. I sat and idly watched the clinic staff as they went about heir jobs and it suddenly dawned on me that all the staff were women, from the eceptionist on up to the doctors. This realization made my cock tingle and swell and squirmed in my seat.

A slim young assistant came out and called my name. I got up and followed her o an exam room. She gave me a short blue and yellow cotton hospital gown and old me to take off all my clothes and put it on. She said someone would be with me n a moment. After I had done as she'd told me I relaxed and let myself enjoy the oft feel of the cotton gown against my skin. Then I sat down on the cold plastic hair and nervously waited.

When I heard the door knob turn I looked up and was surprised to see Jane, the urse practitioner enter. She smiled when she saw me and said she was glad that I ad decided to keep the appointment. She told me that Dr. Brown had asked her to rep me for the exam. She told me to get up on the examination table on my back nd to put my feet in the stirrups.

Jane wheeled over a stainless steel cart and stepped between my legs. She ushed back my gown and began to apply shaving cream all over my genital area. I quirmed and struggled desperately not to become aroused, but my efforts were uitless. I was soon swollen and erect again. Jane laughed softly when she saw that nd told me not to worry, she had expected it. She then proceeded to take a straight azor and carefully shave every square centimeter of my genital area. She seemed to pend a disproportionate amount of time dawdling over my scrotum, being careful o shave it just as close and clean as possible. After she finished shaving it, she took few moments to squeeze and caress the tight, pink, newly hairless sac. I moaned nd squirmed and a big bead of precum oozed out of my cockhead. She giggled and ook a warm wet wash cloth and cleaned off the remaining shaving cream and then ried me with a towel. She then told me I could get down off the exam table and sit ack down in the chair again.

I asked her why it had been necessary to shave me, and she replied that it enerally wasn't strictly necessary, but then again, when it did turn out to be ecessary during the course of the exam it was best to have it all taken care of in dvance, just in case, so there would be no hold-ups or delays. I asked her if she ould be more specific, and she just looked at me with a little twinkle in her eye and

said that everything would become clear to me during the exam and then left.

As soon I was alone again I took the opportunity to lift up my gown and look underneath at my newly shaved genitals. They looked so strange, so bald and exposed. To my horror I found myself becoming stubbornly erect again. I leaned forward in the chair and crossed my arms over my lap to try and hide it.

I heard the door knob turning again and looked up to see a lovely young women in a short white lab coat enter. I was stunned by how healthy and confident and sex she was. She smiled and greeted me and introduced herself as Dr. Brown.

She proceeded to sit down in a chair opposite me and crossed her shapely nyloned legs. I stared at them in mute fascination.

Dr. Brown said, "Now then, Mr. Jones, do you know why you have been asked to come in to see me this morning?"

I responded, "No, ma'am, I'm sorry, but I don't really know exactly why I had to come here today."

"Well I'm glad that you did, Mr. Jones, because its an excellent sign - it shows a willingness to try and work through your problems."

"I'm very happy to cooperate, doctor. I realize you have my best interests at heart. And I'd like to ask you question, if I may."

"And what is that, Mr. Jones?"

"I've never heard of a sexual behavior consultant before. What is it? What do they do, basically?"

"Well, Mr. Jones, the field of sexual behavior management is a new medical discipline that's only begun to grow in the last couple of years. My mentor in medic school, Dr. Veronika van Gelder, is one of the pioneers in the field. And this clinic is one of the first in the country to offer this service. Sexual behavior management deals with recognizing and managing the often unruly sexual behavior of males."

"Oh? Then your patients are exclusively male?"

"That's correct, because they are the ones in the greatest need of help and guidance in this area. But let's get back to your problems, Mr. Jones."

"OK, but could you please explain what exactly my problems are, doctor? I think know what they are but I'm still feeling kind of unsure."

"Of course. Well, as you may recall, on your last visit, while nurse practitioner Jane was examining you, you exposed your erect sexual organ to her. Correct?"

"Yes, doctor, I did and I'm very sorry, I know I shouldn't have."

"Very good, Mr. Jones, the first step in overcoming these problems is to admit hem. By the way, Mr. Jones, why are you sitting like that? Why do you have your rms down and crossed in your lap like that?"

"Oh, oh, doctor, its nothing, I just had to lean forward like this for a while and..."

"Put your arms down at your side and lean back in your chair now, Mr. Jones. 'mon now, don't be shy, do as I say, do it now for the doctor. That's right. Oh my, Ar. Jones, what's that I see tenting your gown up between you legs? C'mon now, ull the gown up to your waist and spread your legs nice and wide so the doctor can ee."

Burning with shame and humiliation I do as I'm told and am soon exposing my ard, swollen cock to the doctor's amused gaze.

"My, my, Mr. Jones, I don't think I've ever seen a case like yours before. You ertainly are quite an excitable boy, aren't you? Tell me, Mr. Jones, do you enjoy xposing yourself to women? Now tell the truth and don't waste my time."

"Yes, doctor, I do like it, I do like to expose myself to women. I'm sorry, but I can't elp it, it just happens all by itself and it feels so good to do it. Oh, please don't be ngry with me!"

"Of course not, of course not, this is a modern clinic, we don't get angry when a atient has a problem. No, no, that wouldn't help solve the problem at all. No, as an xperienced clinician, I know exactly what's called for when a patient behaves as you re doing now."

Meanwhile, as the the doctor and I are talking, I ball and unball my fists and my ands fidget uncontrollably at my sides. Dr. Brown notices this and asks "Why, hatever is the matter with your hands, Mr. Jones? You seem to be having quite a roblem with them. Are you anxious to do something with you hands at this oment, Mr. Jones?"

"Uhhh, yes, oh, uh, yes, doctor, I'd like to, I really feel I have to, I need to do omething really really bad right now..."

"Yes, Mr. Jones, and what would that something be, hmmmmm? I bet I know, I et you have an overpowering urge to get some relief by grabbing your hard cock ith your hand and vigorously pumping it, am I correct?"

"Oh, oh, ah, oh, oh, doctor, oh!" I exclaim as I recklessly and impulsively grab my iff cock just as she's described and start pumping it furiously.

"Stop that! Stop that at once, Mr. Jones! What on earth do you think you're

doing?!?! This is a modern professional medical clinic, not some sleazy massage parlor! Take your hand off your cock at once, do you hear me?!?! At once!!!"

I reluctantly do as instructed and meekly lean back in my chair, blushing and ver ashamed of my flagrant display of uncontrolled lust.

"Alright now, that's quite enough of that foolishness," says Dr. Brown. "I think w should get your treatment program underway immediately, Mr. Jones. Please remove your gown and get into that special treatment chair over on the other side of the room, OK? You have to kneel face forward as you get into it, yes, that's right, and then bend over so your chest and elbows are resting down on the other side. It perfect for the kind of treatment I apply. It keeps the head and chest down, the ass high, and the legs spread wide, giving me complete access to your genitals and rectum."

I get into the chair and feel totally exposed and vulnerable and completely in he power. Dr. Brown examines my genitals and notes aloud that Jane seems to have done an exemplary job for my prepping. She gently runs her hand over my pink, hairless scrotum and says how much she enjoys the sight of a freshly shaved male sac. My cock swells in response and I moan and shudder with intense pleasure.

"Oh, by the way, Mr. Jones," Dr. Brown says, "Jane informed me of your latest sexual indiscretion that occurred while she was prepping you. I'm really beginning t believe that your problem may not be amenable to some of our milder treatment programs. It may turn out to be necessary to apply our stongest treatment alternative."

I hear a rustle of clothes behind me and then some other sounds I can't place.

"But to begin with," says Dr. Brown, "we will start with our intermediate therap It is quite possible that it will be sufficient to get you started back on the road to healthy and appropriate sexual behavior. Let's hope so, anyway. We're going to kee looking on the bright side, OK?"

The doctor walks around in front of me to show me that she's removed all her clothing except her bra and panties and has strapped a big black strap-on dildo around her waist. It juts out from her crotch quite realistically. I gulp again and clench my rectum.

"Here at this clinic, Mr. Jones, we realize that a male has certain needs, certain sexual needs, and we don't deny them, we simply chose our own way of channelin them. For example, virtually all the males that I treat feel a great need for sexual release when I apply this therapeutic anal stimulation tool. For this purpose we ha developed an automated semen extraction machine. Just relax while I slip the suction sleeve over your erection."

Dr. Brown fits the special suction sleeve over my cock and turns on the machine. I oan and squirm involuntarily as I feel the sweet sensations of the pulsing sleeve ıck softly and steadily.

Dr. Brown liberally applies lubrication to my rectum and proceeds to penetrate e slowly. I give out a sharp cry as she gets the head of the dildo past my tight and nder butt hole. She stops and caresses my ass and haunches gently, talking othingly to me and telling me there is no hurry and that I should just relax and cept the penetration.

I relax and I feel the rest of the dildo slowly slide into me until I feel her soft hips essing against my ass.

"That's good, that's good, Mr. Jones, just relax and let it happen, very good, at's a good boy, good boy." She firmly grasps my hips and proceeds to give me a ood fucking while lecturing me about controlling my urges during a medical exam.

She keeps fucking me until I let go and let my cum squirt into the pulsing, sucking eeve. I moan and writhe and grunt and thrust and Dr. Brown chuckles at the nusing spectacle of my unbridled animal lust. After I have finished, she pulls out. ne removes the strap-on and places it in a small stainless steel sink and then puts er clothes back on.

"Can I get up now, Dr. Brown," I gasp.

"Soon, Mr, Jones, but first I have to ask you some questions. How do you feel ow, Mr. Jones? Do you feel more passive and feminine and more appreciative of e female perspective? And furthermore, do you think you'll be able to control your ges a little better from now on? I should add that I don't expect miracles after only e first treatment session, but I do need to see some significant indication of a ositive result so as to justify scheduling subsequent sessions at this treatment vel."

"I'm sorry, doctor," I reply, "I do feel different now. You've opened me up to such citing new feelings. But I feel more likely than ever to surrender to my sex urges."

"Oh dear," says Dr. Brown, "I was afraid of that. Sometimes the intermediate eatments have the opposite effect than intended. Well, Stan... may I call you Stan, the way?"

"Yes, ma'am, of course you can."

"Good, well, Stan, I'm afraid that these latest developments have left me no ernative but to recommend our strongest treatment plan."

"Oh no," I gasp, "please! Don't do that, please! That sounds much too drastic! n't there some other way? Some other alternative?"

"There, there, Stan", says Dr. Brown, as she pats and rubs my butt soothingly. "Calm down, calm down, there's absolutely nothing to be alarmed about. What we're going to do now is a simple, painless procedure that is usually accomplished less than 15 minutes. It's totally safe and completely routine. I perform it on an almost daily basis, and I've done it many, many times. I can practically do it in my sleep. Now hang on while I get Jane."

I wait quietly in my awkward genuflecting-like position and tremble with uncertainty and anxiousness.

Dr. Brown opens the exam room door and calls out, "Jane, please come to the exam room, I'm going to need your assistance. Cancel my 10 o'clock, and bring me hypo of Zylocaine and my surgical kit.

I'm afraid that Mr. Jones needs the full treatment after all.

In a minute Jane enters the room bringing the requested items. I feel the sting o the hypo as its jabbed into the soft flesh immediately adjacent to my scrotum. In a few minutes Dr. Brown asks me, "can you feel when I do this?" and I tell her no, I don't feel anything. "Excellent, we can begin."

I listen to Dr. Brown and Jane working quietly behind me. After a few minutes, Dr. Brown says, "OK, that takes care of the second one. Now I can sew him up and he'll be as good as new, well, better than new, really, hee hee!" Jane joins in and they laugh lightly and merrily. "Now give me some of that gauze padding so I can start bandaging him up," Dr. Brown says.

After she finishes bandaging me up, Dr. Brown tells me I can get up and get dressed. As I get up and gingerly start to get dressed Dr. Brown calmly watches me leaning casually back against the sink counter, her arms crossed over her lovely, swelling bosom. She says "There, there, Stan, now that wasn't so bad, was it? All very quick, simple and painless, wasn't it? And there'll be no more embarrassing incidents during exams, correct?"

I nod mutely to show my agreement and slowly and carefully pull on my underpants.

Dr. Brown writes out a prescription for painkiller medication and tells me I will probably need to take some as the Zylocaine wears off. "My patients tell me they're usually quite sore for a few days but then the discomfort tapers off considerably. S just hang in there and it'll be over before you know it."

"Your patients, Dr. Brown? What do you mean? How many of your patients do you do this to?"

"Its OK, Stan, most patients are a little shocked and indignant after they've bee snipped but they get over it. After all, what's done is done, right? And to answer

our question, all of them, Stan. All my patients end up having to undergo it. That vas one of my mentor, Dr. van Gelder's, greatest discoveries, that all males need to ave it done. And with the proper guidance all males can be made to accept it. It's nly a matter of time. Some accept it sooner than others, that's all. And once it's een done they all thank me. As I know you will too after you've had a chance to xperience the benefits."

As I turn to leave, Jane gives me a little parting wave with one hand and holds her ther hand over her mouth covering a sly smirk. As I glance at her I begin to dimly ecall that during my initial exam, her fingers touched my privates in an nexpectedly soft and caressing manner. But I couldn't be entirely sure. I turn and valk slowly and carefully out of the clinic. I'm completely stunned and unbelieving of vhat happened and I no longer know what to expect any more.

0. SPERM COW FARM

The life of a sperm cow is hard. Naked, we frisk and play in the pasture or lie and nooze in the warm summer sun. We are naked except for the tight chastity nclosing our sensitive sperm teat.

When the milking bell rings we file into the milking barn. We quietly wait our ırn to be strapped down into the milking stocks.

It feels so heavenly to have the tight chastity removed and our tender sperm teat eleased. The lady milker begins by gently stroking and caressing, making it swell to ursting hardness. But there is anxiety mixed with the ecstasy: "Will there be nough?". Soon we must surrender our spurting sperm cream to the milker's firm, ısistent hands. "Will we meet our quota?"

No indication is given during the milking session. But we know sooner or later ach of us will be led to the gelding stocks.

The female owner and staff of Sperm Cow Farm are so cruel and selfish. A poor ttle sperm cow is only as good as his next load of sperm.

The sperm cows all whimper and squirm when they hear the lady vet's car pull ito the barnyard. We know she has come to castrate. The lady vet and the owner ome smiling into the barn. They select one of the sperm cows and lead him to the elding stocks. He sobs and begs them not to do it. They just laugh.

The lady vet sits down on a short stool behind the poor little sperm cow. She rips off her blouse, exposing her big firm breasts and stiff pink nipples. She loves to astrate. We all have to watch. Nonetheless, many of the us become helplessly roused. If our sperm teat were free we would rub it and spill our precious sperm eam all over the barn floor!

Strangely, we all secretly yearn to be castrated even though we also dread it.

31. THE OLD BULL

He was a solid, well-built man in his mid-50s, an 'old bull'.

At the neighborhood bar the old bull met a sly, seductive, 40-ish woman that he'd never seen before. He let her pick him up and take him home. She spoke to a side of him he'd always kept suppressed and hidden.

During the ride to her home she shyly revealed to him she that collected manhoods and instead of being shocked he was fascinated, hypnotized. He felt himself falling under her spell. "And I bet you've got a nice pair," she whispered.

At her home she showed him a room with neatly arranged rows of specimen jar on shelves: her manhood collection. "Whenever I visit this room I like to think of all the men who left their manhood with me."

"Most of them belong to young stallions," she continued, "but I've collected a few from old bulls like yourself. And of course, they're not big bold stallions when they leave, they're sweet little geldings. And when a proud old bull leaves, he's..." she looked at him with a twinkle, "a meek little steer." He blushed and grunted.

"I have to use a large specimen jar for old bulls like you," she said, "because you balls are bigger. Come with me, I'd like to show you the special room where I do it. Oh, and here, carry this large, empty specimen jar, just in case." She winked and he trembled.

In her special room she laughed and told him that men were all such trusting little boys, it was always so easy to get a man to climb up onto her table even though he knows what she's going to do. "I always give them a hot and steamy milking first," she said. She snickered, "Sometimes when I'm feeling mean I make them do it themselves while I watch."

Then she told him she just wanted to take a quick little peek at his manhood. Sh told him to take off his clothes and climb up onto the table. Soon, he was laying on it, his heels up in the stirrups, his legs spread wide, leaving him obscenely naked an splayed open.

She stepped forward and gently squeezed and caressed his full, hairy sac. He fe his cock begin to swell and lengthen. Her fingers softly curled around his aching hardness and began the familiar milking motion. "I was right," she whispered, "you do have a nice pair". Soon, her sly, knowing hands had him squirming and panting.

"What a good little baby bull. Is my little baby bull going to make nice big

quirties for mommy?"

He gasped as he felt her effortlessly take complete possession of his surging, ulsing sex.

"After you make your little squirties, mommy's going to do something very pecial. I'm going to make you my sweet little angel forever." She softly caressed his ght sac. He grunted and thrust his hips up. She purred and watched smugly as he elplessly squirted. He looked up into her eyes with fear and adoration.

Afterwards, she casually spread shaving cream all over his hairy sac and began having it.

"Why... why are you doing that?" he asked somewhat shakily.

"Don't be frightened," she said warmly, "Mommy's just getting her little baby eady".

"Ready?" he squeaked, "Ready for what?"

"Hmmmmm," she purred, "Oh, I bet you know what it is."

"Oh no!" he cried.

"Hmmmmmmmm, oh yes," she purred.

2. THE PERFECT SERVANT

Lady A: I visited Rachel the other evening. Wonderful servant she has. So quiet nd dutiful.

Lady B: Oh yes, George. Well, he's more than a servant. He's her husband.

Lady A: Husband! Really, how odd.

Lady B: Yes, their relationship is a little out of the ordinary. He's her house-usband, actually. Spends all his time at home, cooking and cleaning.

Lady A: That must be very nice for Rachel. How did she meet such a man?

Lady B: Oh, he was always a shy, submissive person. It's not that hard to meet ich men.

Lady A: Oh, I've met a few submissive men myself, but never as much as Rachel's eorge.

Lady B: Well, he wasn't always as docile and obedient as he is now. She had to

work to help teach him his place in their marriage. And strictly speaking, he's not really a man.

Lady A: Not a man?? How is that possible?

Lady B: Well, he's actually now only a neuter. It was this that made him the perfect servant he is today.

Lady A: You don't mean...?

Lady B: Yes, she told him she needed him to undergo a simple procedure to make him more useful and manageable.

Lady A: And he just said yes??

Lady B: Oh no, he resisted at first but she finally made him realize it was something he'd always inwardly yearned for. She took him to a lady surgeon that specializes in it.

Lady A: And how does he feel now?

Lady B: Oh, he's quite grateful. He's as loyal and devoted as a pet dog.

Lady A: All the same, it must have been quite traumatic on the day of the surgery.

Lady B: Oh sure, he was very anxious. But the surgeon has neutered many men and she said it's always the same, once you get them up on the table with their knees up in the air they squirm and beg to be opened up.

Lady A: Oh, how delicious! Such a naughty and scandalous thing! I must arrange to visit Rachel again so I can tease him about it.

Lady B: Yes, it is quite a delicious thrill. But it's really not that uncommon. Quite a few of the households in that neighborhood contain a house husband. I'm thinkin of getting one myself.

33. WALK-INS WELCOME

Early one morning while walking up the street in the new neighborhood I had recently moved into in San Francisco I stopped in front of a large Victorian house that had a half dozen professional services shingles hanging in front. One advertise the services of a Certified Public Castratrix. I couldn't believe what I was seeing and stood with my mouth open, goggling at it. Also on the same shingle it read, "Walk-ins Welcome". Just then an attractive young woman walked up from the opposite direction and stopped a few paces away. She smiled at me and asked if she could

elp. I stuttered that I just couldn't believe the shingle I saw hanging on the house. he said maybe she can help, since it was her shingle. She asked me if I'd like to ome inside so she could explain more about it.

I followed her into the house and down a corridor and into a closed office suite. he led me into a small office on the left side of the suite, took off her suit jacket and ung it up, and sat behind her desk. She invited me to sit down in the chair facing e desk.

"Do you do what I think you do?" I asked shyly.

"Yes," she said, "I'm pretty sure I do. I castrate."

"Do you do it to animals?" I asked.

"Of course," she replied, "but only to male ones like you."

"How many men have you... done?" I asked.

"Quite a few. I've been doing this a number of years now," she replied.

"Are you going to be doing any... today?" I asked with a gulp.

"You mean, besides yourself?" she asked mischievously. I gulped again and she ughed. Then she looked down and consulted her schedule book that lay open on e desk and continued, "Well, in fact I have 4 scheduled for today, and I usually erage about one walk-in a day, so I'll probably be doing at least five."

"Are you the only one who does this?" I asked.

"No," she replied, "there are at least five other castratrixes in the Bay area. I've et a couple of them and we all have a pretty steady stream of clients. Thanks to us, e local eunuch population continues to grow. Ha ha!"

I started to fidget. She noticed and asked me if it was because I was becoming oused. I admitted that it was. She said she wanted to see, and then she instructed e to strip from the waist down. I nervously did as she asked and soon I stood in ont of her, naked from the waist down and with my erection standing out stiffly in ont of me. She looked me over appraisingly and commented that she thought I had ine, healthy set of organs.

"I find it's very useful to monitor my client's sexual responses during an initial nsultation," she said. She smiled wickedly and instructed me to sit back down and slowly masturbate while we talked.

She asked me how long had I found this topic to be sexually arousing. I admitted I d fantasized about it since I was quite young. She asked me if I had ever thought having it done for real. I just blushed and shook my head. "Well, I can definitely

help you out with that. Just relax and trust me and I'll take care of everything," she said. This made me get all the more excited and to stroke myself with increased vigor.

I asked her how she knew when a man was ready to have it done. She said that many of the males who came to her were confused and uncertain and that she wa: always more than happy to help guide them. With the help of her firm guidance th soon came to accept what she decided was best.

She then reached into her drawer and pulled out a slim book of large format photographs and drawings and handed it to me, asking me to look at them. I put it down next to me on the end table to my left and paged through it with my left han my right still busy pumping in my lap. It contained photos of fit young dominant women vigorously sodomizing effeminate men with strap-ons. All the men were portrayed as being both very humiliated and very aroused by this forceful penetration of their most sensitive and intimate spot. I was fascinated by the pictures. I had never seen any that were even half as good. They were very erotic and my cock swelled even more and I stroked even harder.

Noticing my response she said that being stimulated by such pictures was a goc indication that I would be receptive to having it done because submitting to being emasculated by a dominant woman like that was very similar to castration. Furthe she said, any male who exposed his swollen sex organ to her in her office was definitely ready. And masturbating in front of her meant I was probably more than ready, I probably needed it. I gasped and almost stopped stroking my hard cock. Please don't stop, she said with a smile, I'm enjoying the show.

My cock seemed to swell to an even more intense, bursting stiffness and all my sensations began to become centered in my cock. "But ready isn't the same as willing," I managed to gasp.

"Very true," she replied, "but if you ejaculate in front of me then that shows you're not only willing, you're eager."

I hunched forward, my mouth open, my jaw slack, my legs spread brazenly apa displaying myself fully. My fist moved strongly up and down as I felt my orgasm begin to build.

"I'm glad you came to my office today," she said with a wicked smile. "I'm goin to enjoy taking you in the exam room in a couple minutes and giving you what you need."

"But I... but I...", I stammered.

"Many males have sat where you're sitting now and have jerked off in front of me, just as you are. Believe me, when you finish shooting your load you'll see thin

ny way. And to date, no male who openly ejaculated in front of me has left with a ıll ball sac."

By now I was hovering on the edge. She smiled and said quietly, "Go ahead, do it. ou know you're just dying to show me what you can do. And then afterwards we an get started."

The feelings were overpowering. The dangerous, perilous consequences of what I vas about to do overwhelmed me. Even though I knew what I was committing to I ouldn't resist, couldn't hold back. With a great feeling of anguish and dread I tarted to ejaculate with great force. My first spurt shot a yard in the air and they ept coming, spurt after spurt. She leaned forward, watching it all with keen interest nd delight.

As soon as my cock began to deflate and the last dribbles of sperm were oozing ut she stood up and came around the desk, ordering me to stand up. I rose shakily ɔ my feet and she immediately reached over and grasped my slick, deflating cock vith shocking boldness and familiarity. She gave it a sharp yank and told me to ɔllow her. I followed as she led me by my cock. "Watch out for the puddles," she aid lightly.

I followed her mutely out into the hall and then into the adjacent room which vas equipped as a typical medical exam room. She told me to lie down on the exam able and put my feet up in the stirrups.

She got some wet wipes and cleaned the semen off me and then she covered my crotum with shaving cream. I lay still while I felt her slowly and gently shave my crotum completely bare.

I heard a noise from the outer office. Someone was coming in. A sexy young emale voice called out, "Ms. Van Gelder?" The castratrix was wiping my clean-haven scrotum with a wet wipe as she answered, "Yes, Maryanne, I'm in the exam oom. We've got a walk-in. Please go in my office and clean up the floor. I'm afraid here was a fairly messy consultation."

I heard footsteps going into the adjacent office followed by a low whistle and hen a throaty laugh, "My goodness, I should say so! Very messy!"

Ms. Van Gelder went over to the side of the exam room, opened a drawer and ook out a long hypodermic needle. She came back and told me I was going to feel a ttle prick. She then stuck the needle in next to my scrotum and slowly injected me.

"What's in the needle?" I asked.

"Anesthetic," Ms. Van Gelder replied casually.

Just then Maryanne, a very pretty young girl, came into the office and greeted

Ms. Van Gelder. 'Wow!" she exclaimed, "That sure was an awful lot of thick, gloppy sperm on the floor!" The two women laughed quietly.

Then Ms. Van Gelder said, "Maryanne, this is Stan. I met him outside on the sidewalk this morning. He said he was very curious about the services I offered."

"Very curious and very excited," said Maryanne, "to judge by all the sperm he squirted." She giggled at the thought.

"Yes," said Ms. Van Gelder, "it really was quite a show. I'm sorry you weren't he to see it. I know you would've enjoyed it. And I'm pretty sure Stan would have enjoyed showing off for you as well."

"And now you're going to show him exactly what kind of services you offer?" asked Maryanne coyly.

"Of course," responded Ms. Van Gelder. Then, becoming more businesslike, she continued, "Now, as you can see," said Ms. Van Gelder, "I already have him well shaven. And I injected him with anesthetic a couple minutes ago so he should be numbing up pretty soon. Why don't you set up my stand and put the instrument tra on it?"

I began to feel very vulnerable and a little frightened. "What... what are you going to do to me?" I asked timidly.

"I'm going to give you what you so obviously need and want, Stan. You're really quite lucky because I'm about to make your deepest, darkest, sexiest fantasy come true." She then pinched my scrotum and asked me if I could feel anything. When I told her I couldn't she told Maryanne that they could proceed.

As Ms. Van Gelder began to go to work between my legs I asked her what she was doing. "It's really a very simple procedure, Stan. It's exactly the same kind of thing that's routinely done to male animals, such as horses and dogs, every day. An it's done for their own good, to make them calmer and happier. And so will you. So just relax and it'll be over before you know it."

"Is it like a vasectomy?" I asked.

"Yes," she said, "it's a lot like a vasectomy. In fact some of my colleagues often refer to it as a full-strength vasectomy." She laughed quietly and Maryanne giggled

A few minutes later, Ms. Van Gelder said, "OK, let's get him sewed up. He's nice and fixed now like a horny little doggy." She laughed when she saw my worried loo "Don't worry, Stan, you'll soon get used to being a castrated little eunuch."

4. WIFE OF A BIG-BOTTOMED SISSY

This is the story of how my sly wife turned me into a big-bottomed sissy. She egan by feeding me fattening foods and encouraged me to take up sedentary abits. When I began to put on weight she was delighted with my big, plump ottom. She loved to touch it, to caress and play with it.

Then she began to explore the tender cleft in between my bottom cheeks and to lay with my ultra-sensitive hole. She loved seeing my peeny get all hard and stick ut in front when she played with it. She said I couldn't help showing how much I oved having my bottom hole touched.

She would tell me to roll over so she could play with my stiff peeny. She would ube it up and slowly, teasingly take me towards orgasm. She delighted in controlling ne sexually. She loved watching me overpowered by my arousal, squirming and anting, until she brought me to the brink of shameful humiliation: making me elplessly spurt my semen into her wicked, knowing hands.

She began to get more aggressive and invasive exploring my bottom. She began o lube it up and to penetrate it with her finger. At this point, when it was time for ne to roll over, instead of her playing with my peeny, she would tell me to take it in ny own hand and do it while she gently finger fucked me. As I stroked myself she vould tell me what a good little boy I was. Of course she made me go all the way nd subjected me to the intense humiliation of making myself spurt while she mugly watched. I always blushed hotly when she warmly praised me afterwards.

Then one day I found a copy of "Sissy Care" magazine that she had hidden. It was magazine for sly, cunning women whose partners were submissive sissies. I'd ever heard of it before. The pictures and articles were so hot I quickly yanked off ny pants and started jerking off. One article was about a woman who turned her usband into a big-bottomed sissy. She made him submit to being penetrated with er strap-on. She trained him to cum just from begin sodomized. Then she brought ome a gay friend to penetrate him and shoot a big load of hot cum up his plump ss while he whimpered and squirmed.

I was so absorbed in jerking off to this article that I didn't notice my wife nexpectedly coming into the room. I was startled and a little frightened but she just ughed and said, "Well, just look at the naughty little sissy playing with himself!" I lushed hotly with shame and humiliation.

"I, I can't help it!" I whined as I continued to stroke myself.

"Of course not, dear," she said, "go ahead and enjoy yourself. I'm glad you like at magazine." Then she told me her friend, Bernice, had given it to her.

"Oh, yeah, Larry," I said remembering Bernice's husband. He had started to put

on weight a couple years ago, especially on his bottom. "What happened to him, I haven't seen him in a while?"

"Oh, he's still around," smiled my sly wife, "he just doesn't get out much anymore. He's kind of a house husband."

She told me to go ahead and finish the article because it was a good one.

I went back to reading the article and was astonished to read how the sly wife began encouraging her husband to consider the idea of totally surrendering his manhood. With her sly coaxing and guidance he soon grew to accept and even crav the idea. Then she took him to see a lady doctor. The doctor examined him and questioned him and then told his sly wife she thought he was ready for the little operation. The last photo showed the big-bottomed sissy sitting down, naked, his nipples and childish little rubbery penis painted a bright red. His legs were spread wide, prominently displaying his empty scrotum while his wife stood smiling smugl behind him.

I looked up from the magazine, hardly able to believe what I had read and seen. My sly wife just smiled at me and told me to roll over, she wanted to play with my bottom. She told me to reach back and spread my cheeks for her, she wanted to ge up in between. Then she said she forgot her lube and told me to hold that position until she got back. I couldn't help whimpering and squirming while I waited, all ope and exposed. She noticed my shameless wriggling when she came back with the lube and laughed and called me a naughty little sissy and said, "Looks like you can't wait for me to do it!" Then she finally lubed up my hole and gently but firmly penetrated me with her middle finger. As she began slowly thrusting in and out she purred, "Good little sissy, good little sissy". I helplessly panted and wriggled.

She slowly pulled her finger out and wiped it and said, "And I've got a special surprise for you today, honey," she said. "I bought a strap-on!" And I felt her press the head of it against my tender, but receptive opening. Then she fucked me for th first time with a strap-on.

After she got done fucking me she told me to turn over, she knew I would be in great need of milking. As she milked me she told me that Bernice threw a little part for her lady friends once a month. She would make her husband, Larry, serve drink and food totally naked except for a short vest and slippers. At the end of each part she would make him sit on a stool in the middle of the room and put on a special little masturbation show. The ladies would all applaud and cheer when he spurted. Then, a couple months ago, she asked the ladies to come in and be seated as usual Then she lead her husband by the hand into the middle of the room. He was very shy and bashful. He was naked, except for the vest and slippers, but then they saw that his nipples and penis had been painted a bright red. They cheered and applauded because they knew it meant he had had the little operation. When I heard this it made me let go and start spurting while my wife purred praise and

oproval. Then my wife told me that all the ladies had taken turns playing with arry's little red peepee and feeling around between his legs where his manhood sed to be.

A few months later, my wife told me it that now it was time for us to start talking oout having the little operation done. She told me not to be frightened, but she ad made an appointment for us to go and talk to the same lady doctor that had one Bernice's husband.

The lady doctor was very sly and attractive. She told me to strip so she could kamine me. I was very embarrassed because I got an instant erection. She just niled and told me not to worry, that it was a good sign. She told us that it was ovious from my sweet, submissive behavior and my nice plump bottom that I was a erfect candidate for the little operation. When she said this I couldn't help myself, I abbed my cock and started to desperately jerk off. My wife told me to stop being aughty, but the doctor just laughed and said this happened all the time. She told e to go in the bathroom and finish relieving myself where there was lube and aper towels provided for it.

The doctor gave us a loose-leaf binder to look at that contained photos of other en she had done. They all looked so sweet and shy, showing off their altered otch. And they all had the special bright red nipples and peepees. One of the last hotos was of Bernice's husband, Larry.

. YOUNG DAVID ON AUNT ABIGAIL'S FARM

When young David first comes to stay at Aunt Abigail's farm, she gives him a ur. In the barn, David notices a strange metal-frame contraption. Aunt Abigail plains that it's her gelding stocks. "I provide a special castration service, locally. ey're fully adjustable, so they can hold quite a variety of animals", and she looks at avid with a sly twinkle.

Aunt Abigail is in the habit of stripping off and working topless during the midday eat. David can't help sneaking peeks at her big beautiful breasts as they sway and gle, and he can't help getting an erection. When Aunt Abigail catches him staring, quickly looks away, blushing furiously. He sneaks out to the outhouse every ening to give himself some urgent manual relief.

One day, young David spies on Aunt Abigail while in the act of castrating a farm y. The naked farm boy is down on all-fours, strapped into the gelding stocks. Aunt igail sits behind him, bare-breasted, casually doing it. David is shocked but he's o surprised to find himself becoming hotly aroused. Pulling his cock out, he starts gently stroking it, unaware that Aunt Abigail's nieces are close by, quietly atching.

www.ingramcontent.com/pod-product-compliance
Ingram Content Group UK Ltd.
Pitfield, Milton Keynes, MK11 3LW, UK
UKHW022014190726
13853UKWH00005B/1929